#4

# RIVER
# HEIGHTS

# STOLEN
# KISSES

# CAROLYN
# KEENE

**AN ARCHWAY PAPERBACK**
Published by POCKET BOOKS

New York   London   Toronto   Sydney   Tokyo   Singapore

AN ARCHWAY PAPERBACK *Original*

An Archway Paperback published by
POCKET BOOKS, a division of Simon & Schuster Inc.
1230 Avenue of the Americas, New York, NY 10020

Copyright © 1990 by Simon & Schuster Inc.
Cover art copyright © 1990 Doug Grey
Logo art copyright © 1989 James Mathewuse
Produced by Mega-Books of New York, Inc.

ISBN: 0-671-67762-4

First Archway Paperback printing March 1990

10  9  8  7  6  5  4  3  2  1

AN ARCHWAY PAPERBACK and colophon are registered trademarks of Simon & Schuster Inc.

RIVER HEIGHTS is a trademark of Simon & Schuster Inc.

Printed in the U.S.A.

IL 6+

# 1

"Brr!" Brittany Tate shivered and rubbed her bare arms. "I'm freezing!" Turning to the waitress, she said, "I'll have the usual."

The waitress cleared her throat. "The usual what?"

Brittany tossed back her gleaming dark hair and looked at the woman more closely. Obviously she wasn't a regular waitress. Most of the staff at the River Heights Country Club knew what Brittany ordered for Sunday brunch. "One croissant, no jam," she said. "And coffee. Black, please, and *very* hot."

"Juice?" the waitress asked.

"Hardly." Brittany shivered again and smiled a little too sweetly. "It's not exactly a summer day out here on the terrace."

1

The waitress walked away quickly. Brittany felt slightly ashamed of her behavior, but she *was* cold. Something else was bothering her, too: Jack Reilly, her brunch date. Gorgeous freshman at Westmoor University. Country club member. Sensational kisser. And Brittany Tate's boyfriend. She was the envy of almost every girl in her junior class at River Heights High. Brittany should have felt fantastic, but she didn't. She sneaked a peek at Jack and saw a definite frown form between his brown eyes.

"Come on, Brittany," Jack said in a low voice. "She just asked if you wanted some juice. You didn't have to be sarcastic."

"I didn't mean to be," Brittany said. She reached across the glass-topped wrought-iron table and took Jack's hand. "I guess I did sound a little grumpy," she said, giving him a winning, forgive-me smile. "It's the weather, I think. I wish winter would never come. The club is so dull in the winter." She rubbed her arms again, protecting herself against the cool fall breeze. Maybe Jack would scoot his chair over and put his arm around her.

Jack gave her hand a little squeeze, but he didn't move his chair an inch.

Disappointed, Brittany gazed out over the terrace at the velvety green golf course. Not very long before, she'd been worried about

Jack getting *too* close. After the country club dance, when he'd driven her out to Moon Lake so they could really be alone, she'd been a little afraid. She was crazy about Jack, but she wasn't sure how far he wanted their romance to go. His kisses were wonderful, and Brittany couldn't help responding.

Then, just when she'd decided she'd have to tell Jack that things were moving too fast, a police car had driven up. The officers were checking for trespassers and told the two "lovebirds" to move on. Brittany was so glad they'd shown up that she forgot to be embarrassed.

The funny thing was, Jack didn't mind, either. He seemed to sense that she wanted the romance to go more slowly, and he didn't push her. Everything had been wonderful after that, and for a while Brittany was on top of the world.

Then things started to change. Brittany had caught Jack staring at her lately with a puzzled expression. It was as if he couldn't remember who she was. He'd been picking on things she said, too, like her remark to the waitress. Brittany sighed. She *had* sounded sarcastic. She'd have to watch herself.

When the waitress brought their order, Brittany gave her a big smile and thanked her. Then she took a sip of the coffee and burned her tongue. Gasping, she gulped down some water and glanced at Jack. He was actually grinning!

"Well," he said with a chuckle, "you did want it *very* hot."

Brittany forced herself to smile even though her tongue was still on fire. If it had been anyone but Jack, she would have seriously considered dumping the rest of the water on his head. Dousing Jack with water was much too risky, though. She was crazy about him and didn't want to lose him. She'd miss the rides in his sports car, the envious glances of other girls, the dates at all the college hangouts. Last, but certainly not least, she'd miss the country club.

To Brittany, the River Heights Country Club was the top rung on the social ladder. Her own family could easily afford to belong. Well, maybe not *easily,* but they could definitely afford it. Unfortunately, her father, who was a great guy in so many ways, was an absolute mule when it came to joining. He had no interest in golf or tennis; he'd rather spend his spare time puttering in his basement workshop. As far as Mr. Tate was concerned, there was no need for the family to join the country club. Brittany was the only one who was interested in it. Besides, she could always go as a guest with her best friends, Kim Bishop and Samantha Daley. Her father completely missed the point. Going as a guest was fine, but belonging was what counted!

Jack thought Brittany *was* a member. When they'd first met, she thought it would be important to him, so she pretended she belonged. Now she knew that Jack wouldn't care, but she felt it was too late to tell him the truth. She just made sure that he was the one to sign the register whenever they went.

Brittany stirred her coffee and took another, smaller sip. As long as she had Jack, she could be almost completely happy. The important thing was to keep him.

Brittany reached for Jack's hand again, but before she had a chance to take it, he'd lifted it off the table to wave to someone.

Brittany turned in her chair and frowned. Jogging lightly up the terrace steps, a tennis racquet slung over one shoulder, was Nikki Masters.

"Oh, it's Nikki," Brittany said, trying to sound pleasantly surprised.

Jack nodded. "Yeah. She must be taking tennis lessons."

Of course, Brittany thought with disgust. Sweet, golden-haired, blue-eyed, *rich* Nikki Masters. She would be able to afford private lessons. Not only did the Masterses belong to the club, they could probably afford to buy the entire place if they wanted to.

Brittany had another reason for being jealous of Nikki: Tim Cooper, a new guy in their class at River Heights High. At the beginning of the year, Brittany had made a play for Tim and almost won him over. Almost didn't count, though. Handsome, gray-eyed Tim fell in love with Nikki instead. As far as Brittany knew, the two of them were blissfully happy. So why was Nikki at the club with another guy?

Narrowing her eyes, Brittany gave Nikki's companion a once-over. Thick, sun-bleached hair, strong build, and a golden brown tan, even late in the fall. A hunk, definitely.

"Hey, Dustin!" Jack called.

The hunk lifted his racquet and waved it. Then, putting a hand casually on Nikki's shoulder, he guided her toward Jack and Brittany's table.

Brittany made her frown disappear completely and rearranged her face into a warm, welcoming smile. She exchanged polite greetings with Nikki, then waited to find out who this other person was.

"Dustin Tucker, Brittany Tate," Jack said. "Dustin's the club's newest tennis instructor," he told Brittany.

"Newest and best," Nikki said. "He gave me some great tips. I think my game's going to be much better from now on."

"It wasn't bad to begin with," Dustin said

easily. There was admiration in his voice and a sexy twinkle in his dark brown eyes.

"I'm sure Nikki's boyfriend will be happy about that," Brittany said sweetly. There, she thought. Now Dustin knows Nikki's got a boyfriend, in case he had any ideas about dating her. After all, Nikki already had Tim. She didn't need any appreciative glances from Dustin Tucker.

Nikki didn't seem to care, though, much to Brittany's annoyance. "Tim's not that crazy about tennis," she said with a laugh. "In fact, he's only played about three times in his life."

"What about you, Brittany?" Dustin pulled up a chair and sat down next to her, stretching out his powerfully muscled legs. "Do you like the game?"

"Oh, I love it," Brittany said enthusiastically. "I was just telling Jack that I wish winter would never come. I hate it when the courts are closed. There are indoor courts in town, of course, but it's just not the same somehow."

"Right," Dustin agreed with a smile. He really did have sexy eyes, Brittany thought. If it weren't for Jack, she might even be interested.

"Well, hey!" Dustin stood up suddenly. "Nikki's lesson is over, and I don't have any more scheduled. How about a quick doubles match? The four of us?"

"Sounds good to me," Jack said, shoving his plate aside. "I've got my racquet in the locker room. This'll be a good way to work off brunch."

"Fine with me," Nikki said. "How about it, Brittany?"

Brittany was sure the last thing Nikki wanted was to play tennis with *her.* Or was that a knowing glint in Nikki's blue eyes? Could Nikki possibly know the truth — when it came to tennis, Brittany didn't even know which side of the line to stand on.

Oh, she'd hit a ball around a few times with Kim and Samantha, but it would be a miracle if she got the ball over the net.

"Brittany?" Jack was standing up, his mood very cheerful now. "What do you say?"

"Well . . ." Brittany cleared her throat, thinking fast. "It sounds great, but — uh — I don't have my racquet with me." Hah. She didn't even own a racquet.

"No problem," Dustin said with a shrug. "There are plenty of spares in the clubhouse."

Brittany smiled through clenched teeth. "Wonderful," she said. She pushed her chair back, still trying to think of a good way to get out of this. She took her napkin off her lap and got another idea. "Oh, too bad!" she cried, pointing to her short denim skirt. Nikki and Dustin were both in tennis whites. "I'm dressed all wrong."

"No, you're not," Jack said. He was wearing a blue warm-up suit. "That skirt's okay for tennis. And nobody's going to make a fuss just because we're not wearing white."

"Right. This isn't Wimbledon," Dustin agreed.

"Come on, Brittany, it'll be fun." Grinning, Jack took her hand and pulled her to her feet. "Besides, a few minutes ago you were complaining about being cold. This is a good way to warm up."

She was out of excuses. Unless a natural disaster occurred in the next five minutes, Brittany knew she was trapped. She laughed weakly as they left the terrace and headed for the clubhouse. Jack didn't know how wrong he was. The game was going to be a lot of things, but fun was definitely not one of them.

Ten minutes later Brittany took her place on the court. Across the net, Jack gave her a big wave with his racquet. She waved back, still hoping to be saved. Maybe she could fake an injury. Tennis elbow? No, she didn't know what that was. A pulled hamstring? No good. She didn't know *where* it was.

"Everybody ready?" Dustin called from behind her. At least they were on the same side, Brittany thought. And he was a pro. Maybe he'd carry the game and she could just pretend to play.

Dustin served the ball and Nikki returned it. The fuzzy yellow ball seemed to be whizzing straight for the space between Brittany's eyes. Holding her racquet up like a shield, she took a step back and stumbled. The ball pinged off the edge of her racquet and bounced three times before rolling away. Stumbling again, Brittany completely lost her balance and landed in a very undignified sprawl on the hard surface of the court.

"You okay?" Dustin asked, trotting up to her.

Of course she wasn't okay, Brittany felt like screaming. She'd just made a fool of herself, and she had the feeling this was only the beginning. She pasted a smile on her face and nodded at him.

"Good." Reaching down, Dustin took her arm and helped her to her feet.

Brittany forced herself to laugh. "I guess the score's—what? One for them—to nothing?"

"Make that love." Dustin laughed, too, very softly.

"What?" Brittany had no idea what he was talking about.

"Love," he repeated. "You know—in tennis, nothing is love."

He was still holding her arm. Brittany noticed that his hand was very strong, and his arm was beautifully muscled. She liked his hair, too. Thick and blond and sun bleached.

Brittany knew she'd found the perfect cover-up for her clumsiness. What better way to take everyone's mind off her utter inability to play tennis than to make them notice something else? Her total ability to attract guys.

Leaning lightly against Dustin, she turned the full force of her dazzling smile on him. "Isn't that amazing?" she said. "I thought love was everything."

Later, Jack drove Brittany home from the country club in total silence. She thought he must be tired. After all, *he'd* just played a game of tennis. Or tried to.

Settling back against the car seat, Brittany smiled to herself. Her plan had worked amazingly well. Dustin had been completely captivated by her. Nobody seemed to notice that she only swung her racquet about three times during the entire game.

Brittany sighed and realized that she was a little tired, too. Flirting took a lot of energy, but she still had some left for Jack. As they neared her house, she shivered slightly in anticipation: his strong arms holding her tight, his lips kissing her softly. There was no doubt about it, Jack Reilly was the most exciting guy she'd ever known.

As Jack turned the car into the Tates' driveway, Brittany shivered again. She couldn't wait for him to kiss her.

The car lurched to a stop. Jack turned in his seat and stretched out his arm. But instead of holding Brittany, he reached past her and pushed open the passenger door.

"See you, Brittany" was all he said.

**2**

"Tennis with Brittany Tate?" Robin Fisher's huge, dark eyes widened in disbelief. "I'm surprised she didn't try to strangle you with the net."

"I'm not sure she even saw the net," Nikki said with a chuckle, pulling her metallic blue Camaro away from the curb in front of Robin's house. It was Monday morning, half an hour before school started. "Brittany's got a lot on the ball but not when it comes to tennis."

As she headed for their friend Lacey Dupree's house, Nikki told Robin how she'd been roped into playing with Brittany. "It was a disaster for Brittany," she said, shaking her head. "At least the game was."

"I wish I'd been there." Robin grinned and stretched out her long legs. "Seeing Brittany Tate humiliated would just about make my day."

"Oh, she wasn't humiliated," Nikki said. "She was having too much fun flirting with Dustin Tucker to care about how she looked."

"You mean the tennis instructor?" Robin clapped a hand on top of her short dark hair. "Right in front of her boyfriend?"

"Well, you know Brittany," Nikki said.

Robin nodded. "If he's male and halfway handsome, he's fair game."

Nikki laughed as she pulled up in front of Lacey's house. "You've got it."

Lacey was waiting for them on her front porch, wearing a fluffy peach-colored sweater against the autumn morning chill. Her long reddish hair was wound around her head in an intricate braid, but a few wavy tendrils had escaped and curled softly against her pale, freckled face. People who didn't know Lacey well thought she was a little spacey, but behind her dreamy face lurked a brain as sharp as a tack.

That morning, though, Lacey didn't seem distant at all. Her shoulders were back, and her mouth was set in a straight line. As she marched quickly toward the car, her friends saw a determined glint in her light blue eyes.

"I wonder what's up?" Robin whispered to Nikki. "Do you think she had a fight with Rick?" Rick Stratton was Lacey's boyfriend. The two of them had been going together since the beginning of the school year.

"I hope not," Nikki whispered back. "She doesn't look mad, though. She looks——"

"I am completely disgusted!" Lacey announced. "Every time I see this car, I want to scream!"

Nikki looked bewildered. "What's the matter with my car?"

"Nothing!" Lacey waited while Robin stepped out, then squeezed herself into the backseat. "It's perfect. It's a car, that's why I feel like screaming!"

Robin and Nikki couldn't help laughing.

"It's not funny," Lacey said indignantly.

"Oh, Lacey, we know it's not," Nikki said as she put the car into drive and started down the street. "Honestly, we weren't laughing at you. We know how long you've been saving for a car."

"I take it you still don't have enough money," Robin said.

"Hah!" Lacey replied. "The way things are going, I'll be lucky if I have enough when I'm a hundred. By that time my eyes will probably be so bad I won't be able to drive!"

Robin and Nikki didn't laugh this time. Lacey was obviously very upset. The

Duprees were fairly well-off. They lived in a nice house and belonged to the country club, but Lacey's parents believed in working hard, especially for luxuries, like a car.

"Okay," Robin said briskly. "Let's try to figure out how you can get more money, Lacey."

"I've been doing that for weeks," Lacey said. "The only thing I can come up with is giving up being junior class secretary."

"What?" Nikki frowned at her in the rearview mirror. "Why would you want to do that?"

Lacey sighed. "Maybe then I could get a second job." She already had one job at Platters, a record store in the mall, but she got paid only minimum wage.

"Two jobs? That's too much," Robin said. "Your grades might slide, and you'd have to give up one of them, and then you'd be back where you started. Except you wouldn't be junior class secretary anymore."

"How about a garage sale?" Nikki asked. "If you organized it, maybe your parents would let you keep the profits."

Lacey smiled ruefully. "It's a good idea, Nikki, but we had one over the summer."

"You're really good in French," Robin said. "I bet you could earn extra money tutoring."

"That's sort of like a second job, though," Nikki pointed out. "It doesn't pay much, either."

"It pays peanuts," Lacey said flatly. "I'm sorry, guys. I know you're trying to help, but I've already thought of just about everything."

Nikki caught Robin's eye as she turned down the long drive toward River Heights High. She knew they were thinking the same thing: they could offer to lend Lacey some money. Nikki's family gave her a generous allowance. Even though Robin didn't have a job because she spent all her free time working out with the swim team, she did have some money saved.

Without saying anything, Nikki and Robin came to the same conclusion: Lacey would borrow money in an emergency, but she'd never take a loan for a car.

As Nikki began searching for a parking space, Robin turned around in the seat and faced Lacey. "Okay," she said. "There's only one thing to do. You have to ask for a raise. Lenny Lukowski pays you peanuts at that record store, and I'll bet he's raking in millions."

"But . . ." Lacey looked doubtful.

"But nothing," Robin broke in. "Okay, maybe the guy doesn't make millions, but business is good, isn't it?"

"Yes," Lacey agreed. "But I told you, Lenny is really tight with money."

"You've been working there for months without a raise," Nikki countered.

Lacey nodded. "Lenny said I'm the best salesperson he's got, and he wishes I'd stay in high school forever."

"There!" Robin cried triumphantly. "You can't lose. He might be tight, but he wouldn't want you to quit on him."

"I guess I could try it," Lacey said thoughtfully. Then she broke into her first real smile of the day. "I'll do it!" she said.

Nikki finally pulled into a parking space. The three of them got out of the car and headed toward the school. The quad was filled with students milling around, waiting for the first bell.

Nikki spotted Tim Cooper on the steps, waving to her. Even from a distance she could tell that his deep gray eyes were sparkling. She waved back happily. Then she remembered: that day was the day they had final fittings for their costumes.

She and Tim were the young, romantic leads in the drama club's production of *Our Town*. Nikki was excited about the play but also very nervous. A few times lately she'd awakened in the middle of the night, her heart pounding in fear.

It wasn't just preperformance nerves,

though, Nikki knew. During the past summer the boy she'd been dating had been killed. For a few horrible weeks, Nikki had been suspected of murder.

Of course, she hadn't been involved at all, and her friend and next-door neighbor, the detective Nancy Drew, had quickly cleared her of the crime.

Now with the play coming up, Nikki's name was starting to appear in the local paper again. Practically every story mentioned the murder. She'd thought the whole thing was behind her, but now here it was, starting up again. She wasn't sure she could face it.

"Nikki?" Robin said.

Nikki shook the disturbing thoughts away. "Sorry," she said. "My mind was wandering. What did you say?"

"I asked if you'd seen Cal," Robin said, "my boyfriend, remember?"

"Not yet." Nikki smiled. "It's nice not to be avoiding him anymore, isn't it?"

With a laugh, Robin agreed. A few weeks earlier she'd had a real scare—she thought she was pregnant. Before she found out she definitely wasn't, she'd kept as far away from Cal as possible so she wouldn't have to tell him what was going on. In fact, they'd almost broken up. Everything was fine now, though.

"Don't worry," Nikki said. "Cal will find you." She stared pointedly at Robin's yellow corduroy pants, blue suspenders embroidered with ladybugs, and orange trapezoid earrings. Then she grinned. "I mean, the guy hasn't gone color blind lately, has he?"

"Very funny," Robin said.

"You *are* dazzling this morning," Lacey teased. Then she waved to Rick Stratton, who was walking across the quad from the parking lot.

Lacey's boyfriend was easy to spot. His hair was medium brown, and he was only medium-tall, but he was built like a linebacker with broad shoulders and solid, muscular legs.

Lacey started toward him, but then she stopped and turned back to Nikki and Robin. "Tell me again," she said.

"Tell you what?" Nikki asked.

"How easy it's going to be to get a raise," Lacey explained.

"We didn't say it would be easy to *get* one," Robin corrected her. "We only said it'll be easy to ask for one."

"Right," Nikki said. "Be honest and straightforward. That's the best way."

Lacey took a deep breath. "Okay," she said. "I'll do it today, after school, the minute I get to the record store." She said goodbye to her friends and drifted off to join Rick, repeating to herself out loud, "Honest and straightforward. Honest and straightforward."

As Lacey Dupree passed by, Brittany Tate peered after her, frowning slightly. She rarely paid attention to anything that girl said or did, but Lacey's words caught her ear just then.

Honest and straightforward, Brittany thought. What kind of ridiculous babble was that? It might work for sweet little Lacey Dupree, whatever she was talking about, but it certainly wouldn't work for Brittany Tate.

If she wanted to be honest and straightforward, she'd call Jack and ask him why he'd dropped her off the day before like a load of rotten fruit. And why he hadn't called her that night. Or why he hadn't picked her up for school. She'd had to take the pokey, tacky school bus.

Unfortunately, Brittany had a sneaking suspicion why, and she didn't really want Jack's honest and straightforward answer.

Sighing, Brittany remembered how clever she thought she'd been — turning on every charm she possessed with Dustin Tucker so nobody would notice her total lack of tennis ability.

The plan had worked beautifully, but maybe it had worked too well. Her flirting had been an act, of course, but maybe Jack had taken it seriously. Dustin sure had. When they left, he'd murmured, "If you're ever interested in a singles game, Brittany, I'm available." She knew he wasn't talking about tennis, either. Brittany wasn't sure whether Jack had heard it or not.

She couldn't help but feel worried, and she was so deep in thought she gasped when Samantha Daley put a hand on her arm.

"My goodness," Samantha drawled in her soft southern voice. "You're as jumpy as grease on a griddle. What's on your mind?"

Kim Bishop, who was with Samantha, laughed. "Jack Reilly, who else?" She gave Brittany a sharp glance with her blue eyes. "What are you doing here so soon, anyway?" she asked. "You and Jack usually sit in the parking lot until the warning bell."

Brittany forced a smile as the three of them headed for the main door. "Jack's got a horrible schedule this week—three exams and some big history project that's due soon. So I didn't want to distract him," she said suggestively.

Samantha shook her head, her curly, cinnamon brown hair swinging gently. "Poor Jack."

"Poor Brittany," Kim said.

"Poor both of us," Brittany corrected her. They all laughed together, and Brittany started to feel better. Why tell Kim and Samantha what had happened? Jack might be a little annoyed with her right then, but he couldn't possibly be angry. He knew she was wild about him, and he *was* busy. The part about the history project was true. She'd just wait until he called, and then she'd make everything all right again.

# 3

Determined not to worry about Jack *yet,*
Brittany left her two friends in the main hall
and headed for the newspaper office. DeeDee
Smith, the editor of the school paper, the
*Record,* had been bugging her to come in and
discuss her column before their first class.

She really didn't understand why DeeDee
was in such a big rush. Brittany's regular
column, "Off The Record," was the most
popular part of the paper. Music, fashion,
trends—Brittany covered them all. The
whole school read her column as if its words
were carved in stone. So what if she sometimes got it in a little late? Good things were
always worth waiting for.

As she walked into the newspaper office,

Brittany spotted DeeDee. She was hunched over a desk next to Karen Jacobs, the layout and production editor, going over that week's edition. Karen saw Brittany first and gave her a small smile.

Small-boned, Karen always dressed in muted colors—dusky blues, soft grays, light browns—and pulled her hair back in a clip. To Brittany, who was dressed that day in a silky purple blouse and elegant, winter white corduroy pants, Karen looked like a timid, nose-quivering rabbit. Her only good feature was her eyes, which were large and hazel-green, but they were ruined by wire-rimmed glasses that were much too big for her face.

Even though Karen acted like a timid rabbit, Brittany knew the girl was smart and ambitious. She also knew that Karen didn't like her much. Jealousy, Brittany thought. She gave Karen a quick smile and focused her attention on DeeDee, an attractive black senior.

"Well, well, it looks like our hotshot reporter is ready to work," DeeDee remarked.

Brittany decided to ignore the sarcasm. DeeDee *was* the editor-in-chief, after all. Anyway, she was a senior. Next year, if all went right, Brittany would be the one ruling the paper.

"Yes, I'm here, and I've decided what to

put in next week's column," Brittany announced. She'd only thought of it during her walk down the hall, but so what? She worked best under pressure.

"Well?" DeeDee said. "What is it?"

"The Dead Beats," Brittany replied.

"Dead Beats?" Karen echoed thoughtfully.

Brittany gave her a pitying look. "They're a new rock group," she explained sweetly. "They're not that well-known yet, but I have a feeling they're going to be really big."

"Oh, I've heard of them," Karen said. "In fact, they're doing a publicity tour of the Midwest right now, to promote their first album."

This was news to Brittany, but she didn't let on. She was mildly amazed that Karen knew, though. Brittany figured she only read things like *Time* and *Newsweek.*

"Anyway," Karen went on, "it would be great if you could get an interview with them."

"Great?" DeeDee broke in excitedly. "It would be fantastic! What about it, Brittany?"

"Well . . ." Brittany didn't want to tell them what a ridiculous idea it was. The Dead Beats weren't world famous yet, but they were definitely on their way. They'd hardly have time to talk to somebody from River Heights High. DeeDee *was* the editor, so

Brittany decided to play along, even though it was hopeless. "I suppose it could be possible," she said slowly. "I'll check into it, but it might not make next week's column. It really is a long shot." About as long as a football field.

"Maybe not," Karen said. "The article I read said they were hoping this tour would put the Dead Beats on the map. That must mean they'll be looking for as much publicity as they can get." She pushed her glasses up on her nose and smiled at Brittany. "I'll be glad to give you the article. It had the name of their manager and a list of all the towns they were touring, plus the dates."

"Good," DeeDee said decisively. "Take the article and give it your best shot, Brittany."

"Sure," Brittany agreed.

"Oh, and one more thing," DeeDee said. "Karen came up with another idea."

"Oh?" Doing the column on the Dead Beats had been *her* idea, Brittany thought in annoyance. All Karen had done was make it more difficult.

DeeDee nodded. "We've done a few stories on *Our Town,* but Karen thought it would be interesting if we did another one on the leads — you know, an up-close-and-personal sort of thing."

Stifling a yawn, Brittany tried to look

impressed. "Great idea, Karen," she said. "Good luck with it."

"No, Karen doesn't have time," DeeDee said. "I'd like you to handle it, Brittany."

"Me?" Brittany would rather have handled a dead rat than an interview with Nikki Masters and Tim Cooper. "I'm not sure I'll have the time, either."

DeeDee gave her a sharp glance. "Look, Brittany, Karen and I are up to our ears in work right now, and there's nobody else on the paper who can do the article."

Karen and I? DeeDee was talking as if she and Karen were coeditors or something. Brittany looked from one girl to the other and a suspicious thought leaped into her mind. Could Karen possibly be hoping to take over as editor of the *Record* next year? After all, the outgoing editor's recommendation carried a lot of weight. Of course, they'd both have to be page editors before they'd be qualified for the job. Brittany was aiming for that position next semester, but Karen might be, too.

Well, if that was Karen's plan, she could forget it. Brittany hadn't worked all this time on the paper to let some rabbity layout editor show her up. And if she had to interview Nikki and Tim, then fine. She might gag when she wrote it up, but she'd do it.

"Sure, DeeDee," she said as enthusiastically as possible. "It sounds like a great story. I'll get right on it. When do you want it in?"

DeeDee looked her straight in the eye. "Before the play opens, Brittany. Okay?" With that, she and Karen turned back to the papers spread out on the desk.

Brittany had obviously been dismissed, and she didn't like that one bit. She also didn't like the idea that Karen might be after the editor-in-chief position. Not that she'd get it, of course, but it was just one more headache for Brittany, on top of Jack. Because in spite of deciding not to think about him, she hadn't been able to get him off her mind.

Brittany had hoped her run-in with DeeDee and Karen would be the low point of her day. Unfortunately her day went downhill from there. When school was finally over and she headed for her locker, Brittany was frazzled and extremely frustrated with life in general.

Peering into the mirror that she'd taped to the inside of her locker door, Brittany saw that she looked frazzled, too. She whipped out a tube of lipstick and began to repair the damage, reflecting on her lousy experiences.

First, there was lunch. Brittany's table was almost always the center of attention, with people dropping by to talk or see if she might have time to work on some committee or other.

That day, though, it was extremely boring. Nobody even seemed to notice she was there. When she'd said something about it, Kim had been her usual blunt self. "You're not exactly in the swim of things here at school anymore, you know," she pointed out. "You're always off with Jack at some college hangout."

Brittany had laughed it off at the time, but now, as she ran a brush through her gleaming dark hair, she wondered if Kim were right. By spending so much time with Jack, was she letting her grip on the River Heights High social scene slide?

No, that was impossible. Brittany had always been at the center of things. It would take an earthquake to dislodge her. Besides, Jack was a social plus, she thought. Or was. No, *is*.

As she was smoothing her eyebrows with the edge of her brush, Brittany noticed Nikki Masters hurrying by. Probably on her way to rehearsal, she thought. Which was another thing that had made the day less than perfect.

After lunch Brittany gritted her teeth and asked Nikki and Tim about the stupid *Our Town* article. Tim had been eager to do it, but

Nikki seemed reluctant. The girl wouldn't give Brittany a definite date for an interview.

Imagine! A chance to be half the story in a feature article and Little-Miss-Have-It-All decides to be modest. "The play's the important thing," Nikki had said. "Not the people in it."

Well, Brittany thought, that was fine. If Nikki kept on being difficult, she'd bury her so deep in the story that people would need a magnifying glass to find her name.

The thought made Brittany extremely happy, and the sight of her smiling reflection, perfect once more, cheered her up, too. Slamming her locker, Brittany walked confidently down the hall and out of River Heights High.

At almost the same time, Lacey Dupree marched down the long corridor toward the record store at the mall. But in spite of telling herself over and over that she deserved a raise, Lacey wasn't sure Lenny Lukowski would agree with her. Still, she had nothing to lose. He certainly wouldn't fire her for asking.

She paused at the store window, smoothed a few straying tendrils of hair, and nodded to herself. "Honest and straightforward," she whispered once again. Then she pushed open the door and went inside.

Lenny Lukowski was in his usual place

behind the counter, ripping open a shipping box of compact discs. He was in his thirties, with shiny dark hair and eyes to match. Seeing Lacey come in, he stopped opening the box and leaned on the counter, his fingers automatically tapping out a beat.

"Lacey, good," he said around the wad of gum in his mouth. "You can start pricing this new shipment now."

Lacey took off her sweater and folded it into the cubby behind the counter. "I'll get on it in just a few minutes, Lenny."

The fingers stopped tapping. "A few minutes?" he repeated. "Lacey, the after-school crowd is about to descend. Don't you think we should get these CDs out so the kids can snap them up here instead of going to another store?"

Lacey nodded. "I know, Lenny," she agreed. "I'll get them priced fast—don't worry." She started to sit on the high stool behind the counter, then changed her mind. Sitting might make her seem weak. Throwing back her shoulders, she stood up straight and said, "I need to talk to you, Lenny. I want to ask you for a raise."

Brittany's confidence lasted until she stepped outside and scanned the parking lot. Then her heart sank like a stone. No familiar car was waiting for her, no brown eyes were smiling at her from the driver's window, no strong hand was waving to her. Jack wasn't there.

Of course, he didn't always pick her up after school, but it was Monday, and Monday was the one day he always did.

Licking her lips, Brittany forced herself to smile before starting down the steps. Her chin was high, and she knew she looked great. Appearances counted. Nobody needed to know that she felt like tossing her books down, stomping on them, and shrieking at the top of her lungs.

Just keep calm until you get home, she told herself. Maybe Jack will call you then. Maybe he's already called and left a message.

A car horn sounded suddenly. Brittany had been so busy willing herself to stay cool that she jumped half a foot in the air. Her heel caught on the last step and she teetered on the edge, waving her arms for balance. She managed to stay upright, but her books flew out of her hands and scattered on the pavement below.

"Sorry about that," a voice said, not sounding sorry at all.

The car was a sleek, black Porsche, and the driver was Jeremy Pratt.

Smooth, cultivated, and very good looking, Jeremy came from one of the wealthiest families in River Heights. As far as Brittany was concerned, he might as well have come from a nest of vipers.

"I wish you wouldn't sneak up on me like that," Brittany said crossly, kneeling down to retrieve her books.

"But, Brittany, it's the only way I can get to see you these days." Jeremy looked down his nose and smiled. He's being sly, Brittany thought. "I get the feeling you've been hiding from me lately. I wonder why."

"Don't be ridiculous. I've just been busy," she told him. It was true, but not entirely. She *had* been avoiding him.

"Ah, but not too busy to play tennis and enjoy brunch at the country club," he pointed out. "Right, Brittany?"

"Right, Jeremy, but——"

"We made a bargain," he cut in smoothly. "So far, you haven't kept your side of it." Jeremy leaned across the front seat and clicked open the passenger door. "Get in, Brittany. I think it's time we talked."

Brittany realized she was trapped. Jeremy always collected on his bargains.

With a sigh, she straightened up and walked the few steps to the car. Oh well, she thought, at least she'd get to ride in a Porsche.

"So that's it, Lenny," Lacey concluded. "I honestly think I deserve a raise. I've been working here since the beginning of school, I'm very responsible, and you said yourself I'm the best person you ever hired."

There, she thought with relief. She'd done it. And she thought her case was pretty strong. In fact, she didn't know how he could possibly turn her down.

Lenny had given her his full attention, not interrupting once. Now he started tapping his fingers again and grinned at her. "You still haven't saved enough for that car you're dying to have, huh?"

The man had the memory of an elephant, Lacey thought. She'd deliberately avoided mentioning the car because she didn't think it would matter *why* she wanted a raise.

"I know, I know, what you want the raise for is none of my business," Lenny said. "You're right, it isn't."

He stared at his hands. Was he thinking it over seriously? Lacey wondered. Was this a good sign?

"Everything you said is true," Lenny told her.

Lacey tried not to get her hopes up.

"But you've got to understand something," Lenny said. "I can't just up your wage. I mean, I hired you for minimum and you said okay. If you want more money, you've got to play a bigger part in the business."

"I'm willing to take on more responsibility," Lacey told him.

"Yeah? Well, good, because I've been thinking, Lacey. Business isn't bad——"

Lacey laughed, interrupting him. "Come on, Lenny, business is great."

"Well, it can always be better, right?" She nodded. "What I'm looking for is something spectacular," Lenny went on. "An idea that'll get people lined up three deep outside this place. Come up with something that'll do that, and then we'll talk money again."

Before Lacey had a chance to respond, the

door swung open and a huge group of kids poured into the store.

Lacey immediately went to work. As she unloaded and priced the compact discs, straightened up the record bins, and helped out at the cash register, she thought about what Lenny had said: an idea so spectacular they'd have to beat the crowds away.

A sale, maybe? Prices slashed, one day only? No, all the record stores did that.

Spend twenty-five dollars or more and get a free T-shirt or poster? But you could get rock posters and T-shirts just about anywhere, for a lot less than twenty-five dollars.

"Excuse me." A girl interrupted Lacey's thoughts. "Do you have the Dead Beats' new album in yet?"

"Not yet," Lacey said. "Nobody does."

"I know." The girl sighed in frustration. "When's the album going to be released?"

Lacey shook her head. "I'm not sure, but I know they're doing a big publicity tour of the Midwest right now. They'll probably release the album as they go. You know, sort of city by city."

The girl's eyes widened in excitement. "Hey, do you think they'll come to River Heights?"

Laughing, Lacey shook her head again. "Chicago, definitely, but not River Heights. It's way too small."

"Just once I'd like to see a decent group pay attention to small towns," the girl complained. "They only hit the big cities. It's like they don't even know we exist, you know?"

Lacey didn't answer. Her mind was racing. She excused herself and sped through the record aisles. Whirling past a life-size cardboard cut-out of Michael Jackson, Lacey practically screeched to a halt at the counter.

"Lenny!" she said breathlessly. "I've got it!"

He looked up in surprise. "You have what?"

"That spectacular idea you were talking about!" Lacey told him excitedly. "How about this?" She struck a dramatic pose and pretended to read an imaginary newspaper headline. "Dead Beats Arrive in River Heights. Exclusive Autographing Session at Platters Records!"

Smoothly shifting gears, Jeremy turned a corner and pointed the Porsche in the direction of the River Heights Country Club.

"I thought we'd take a little spin by the place," he said to Brittany. "Just to remind you of all the things you might miss out on if you don't keep your end of our deal."

Jeremy's part of the deal had been promising not to tell Jack that Brittany wasn't a member of the club. She should have known he wouldn't let her get away with it forever.

Brittany decided to take the offensive. "You sound ridiculous, Jeremy. Like you're playing the bad guy in a really lousy TV movie."

Jeremy laughed almost soundlessly. "All right, all right. No more heavy," he said. "But we still have to talk."

"I don't see why." Brittany pouted. "I asked Kim to go out on a date with you, and she said yes." That was Brittany's end of the bargain—to get Kim to date Jeremy.

"Yes," Jeremy agreed. "I've called her twice, though, and she's been busy both times."

Brittany shrugged. "So? That's not my fault."

"The second time," Jeremy went on, "she said she'd have to think about it."

Oh, great. Had Kim changed her mind? "Can I help it if Kim takes a long time to think about things?" Brittany asked.

"I think you can." Jeremy glanced over at her, smiling slyly. "You promised to do your best, Brittany, and I get the feeling you haven't."

"All right, all right," Brittany said crossly. "I'll mention it to her again."

"You do that, Brittany," Jeremy said. "And this time, put a little effort into it, okay?"

"Yes!" she said in exasperation. "*Now* will you drive me home? I'm really not in the mood for riding around."

"Not even around your favorite place?" Jeremy nodded toward the vast clipped fairways of the country club golf course.

Brittany scowled at him suspiciously. "What's your point, Jeremy?"

"No point," he said, keeping his eyes on the road. "It's just that if you could manage the membership fee, the rest might be easy."

"What do you mean, 'the rest'?"

"Well, you know that the club has decided to open its membership to five junior members," Jeremy explained. "But you need two sponsors." He turned his head and smiled. "Jack thinks you're already a member, so he's out as one of your sponsors, obviously."

"Obviously," Brittany snapped.

"But Kim and I . . ." Jeremy's voice trailed off, and he gave her a meaningful look.

Brittany scowled at him again, but Jeremy only laughed nastily as he turned the car around and headed back to town.

After Jeremy finally dropped Brittany off at her house a few minutes later, she sauntered up to the front door as if she'd just come home from a delightful drive. Inside, she felt like snapping the head off each and every chrysanthemum lining the front walk.

That creep! That slimy, no-good, sneaky creep! Jeremy knew how much she wanted to join the club, and now he was using it as bait.

"Hey, was that a Porsche?"

Brittany stopped at the bottom step of the porch and frowned. Standing in the doorway was her thirteen-year-old sister, Tamara.

"Yes, it was a Porsche," Brittany snapped, staring in disapproval at Tamara's beat-up jeans and sloppy T-shirt. She wished her little sister would take more interest in her looks than in cars and computers. Tamara had Brittany's same thick, dark hair and sweetly curved mouth, but she hid her attractiveness behind foot-thick glasses. Brittany had been giving the kid some pointers about her hair, but she hadn't been able to talk her into contacts yet.

"Wow," Tamara said, digging into the bag of potato chips she was carrying. That annoyed Brittany, too. Tamara never gained weight, and her face never broke out. "So whose was it?" Tamara asked.

Tamara saw entirely too much through those hideous glasses, Brittany decided. "It was just a friend from school who gave me a lift. Not," she added, "that it's any of your business."

"Oh, good. For a minute there, I was afraid you might be going out with somebody else besides Jack." Tamara had developed an irritating crush on Jack Reilly the minute she laid eyes on him.

"Well, I'm not," Brittany said.

"Okay." Looking relieved, Tamara turned to go.

"Wait." Jeremy's little "talk" had almost made Brittany forget the most important thing. Trying to keep her voice light, she asked, "Did Jack call, by the way?"

"I don't know. I just got home five minutes ago." Tamara stuffed another handful of chips into her mouth and headed toward her room and her precious computer.

Don't panic, Brittany ordered herself. He probably called and nobody was here to answer.

She went into the kitchen and glared at the silent phone. Why didn't her family have an answering machine, like ninety-eight percent of the civilized world?

As she set her books on the kitchen table, the ear-splitting whine of an electric saw came shrieking up from the basement. She'd forgotten. Her father came home early on Mondays. Her teeth on edge from the noise, Brittany went to the door and waited until it stopped.

"Daddy?"

There was a clunk and a thud, and then Mr. Tate appeared at the bottom of the stairs. His face and hair were sprinkled with sawdust. "Hi, sweetheart."

"Have you been using that saw for long?"

Mr. Tate checked his watch. "About an hour, maybe. I decided to repair this old workbench before it collapses on me."

"Oh. Well," Brittany said, "then I guess you wouldn't have heard the telephone, would you?" Fat chance.

"Afraid not," he agreed cheerfully. "Did you just get home? How's Jack?"

"Oh, fine!" Brittany lied. Her entire family adored Jack Reilly. If he didn't call or come by soon, they'd start asking why. At least her mother was still at the mall, working at Blooms, the flower shop she owned, so Brittany wouldn't have to put up a front with her. Yet. "Well, Daddy, I'll let you get back to work," Brittany said lightly.

In a moment the saw started screeching again. Brittany grabbed a diet soda and escaped to her room. Once there, Brittany undressed, slipped into a midnight blue velour caftan, and flopped down on her bed. Earlier, she'd wanted to scream the house down in frustration, but now she decided that screaming would be a waste of energy.

After a day like the one she'd just gone through, she needed every ounce of energy she possessed.

First, DeeDee Smith and Karen Jacobs. Well, that shouldn't be too difficult. She'd simply overwhelm those two with an incredible article on Tim and Nikki. And while they were still gasping in admiration, she'd casually mention that the Dead Beats were unavailable for an interview.

Next, Jeremy Pratt. Harder, but nothing she couldn't handle. Kim didn't really date as much as she could. She was awfully picky when it came to guys, and she'd probably had second thoughts about Jeremy. Brittany didn't blame her for that. Still, the point was to get Kim and Jeremy together for at least one date. Not even Kim would be able to resist a guy she thought was madly in love with her, Brittany decided, scheming. And if the date went well, she'd have her two sponsors for the club. Finally, to be a full-fledged member of the River Heights Country Club! For that, she'd make a bargain with a dozen Jeremy Pratts.

At last, Brittany thought of Jack. Her eyes strayed to her bedside phone. It was just sitting there, a silent lump of white plastic.

Should she call him? It was obvious now that Jack was angry. What would happen if she just picked up the phone, explained why she'd flirted with Dustin, and apologized? Nice and simple, right?

Wrong. Jack already knew something about her that she'd tried to keep secret: the fact that her mother ran a flower shop. Brittany wasn't ashamed, exactly. Her mother did a great job. But people who belonged to the country club *ordered* flowers, they didn't sell them. When Jack had found out, he'd been pretty mad. He couldn't understand why she'd lied to him about her mother's job.

If she apologized for flirting with Dustin now, Jack would want to know why she'd lied about playing tennis. That might make him wonder how she could possibly be a member of the country club all these years and not know how to play. Then the whole truth would come out, and she would look as if she were only interested in Jack because he was a college man and a member of the club.

That was partly true, Brittany had to admit. But she would never have schemed or lied if she weren't totally crazy about him. Still, how could she possibly explain everything?

Brittany sat up, took her brush from the night table, and pulled it through her hair. Calling Jack would be a mistake. Things were already complicated. Why muddle them up even more with the truth?

Besides, Brittany made it a point never to go crawling and begging for forgiveness. The very thought made her shudder. There were better ways to get what she wanted. She'd think of something. She always did.

**5**

"Come on, Lacey—the Dead Beats?" Lenny said, shaking his head. "I mean, you're talking about the impossible."

"No, I'm not," Lacey insisted. She'd spent the last half hour following him around the store, trying to talk to him between customers. She was getting very tired of his negative attitude.

The store was empty for the moment, and Lenny was leaving early that day. Lacey knew that if her boss left now and had too much time to think about it, he'd tell her to forget the whole thing.

"Listen to yourself, Lenny," she said. "You asked for a spectacular idea that would make Platters famous and leave all the other

47

stores in the dust. I just gave you that idea.
And what do you do? Tell me it's impossi-
ble!" Lacey stopped and took a deep breath.
"Don't you see how fantastic the Dead Beats
will be for business? That new store at the
other end of the mall will never catch up.
And I can get the Dead Beats here, Lenny!
Right here in Platters!"

Lenny seemed amazed at the speech.
Lacey was a little amazed herself, but she
decided she could do it.

"Look!" Lacey poked a finger at a page in a
rock magazine on the counter. "See? Accord-
ing to this, the Dead Beats will be in Chicago
next week."

Lenny peered at the article. "Yeah. So?"

"So Chicago isn't that far from here,"
Lacey reminded him. "And their whole promotion is about 'getting in touch with the
country.' There's a lot more to this country
than just the big cities. How could they
refuse a little side trip to River Heights?"

"Seems like they couldn't," Lenny admitted. "But how are you planning to pitch this
little side trip to them?"

Lacey pointed to the magazine again.
"Here's their manager's name and number."

"You mean you're just going to call her
up?" Lenny asked.

Lacey nodded impatiently. "It's New York,
though, and there's the time difference, so

I'd better do it right now." She turned away and headed for the office. "You don't mind if I use the phone, do you?"

"Well, I—"

"Don't worry, Lenny," Lacey called back over her shoulder. "I know it's long distance." Stopping at the office door, she turned and grinned at him. "It's okay. You can deduct it from my raise."

"You're really determined to do this?" he asked.

"I sure am."

Lenny still didn't look convinced, but he finally nodded. "Okay, Lacey," he said. "If you get the Dead Beats into this store, you've got yourself a raise."

"By the way, Brittany, what's happening with the Dead Beats?"

Brittany glanced up from her lunch tray the next day and saw DeeDee Smith standing next to her in the line. Beside DeeDee was Karen Jacobs. Like a shadow, Brittany thought in irritation.

"Happening?" Brittany said casually. She racked her brain, trying to remember what the article in that rock magazine had said. She'd only scanned it. "Well—"

Karen cleared her throat. "They'll be in Chicago next week, I think. Isn't that right?"

"Right," Brittany agreed. It could have been next year, for all she knew. "A little too late for my column, I'm afraid."

"Maybe not," Karen said. "They'll be in Chicago on Wednesday, and they leave on Saturday." She turned to DeeDee. "Brittany might be able to get something in time. The *Record* doesn't come out until Friday."

"And how do you suggest I 'get' something?" Brittany asked sweetly. "Cut school and go to Chicago in the middle of the week?"

Karen shook her head, ignoring Brittany's sarcasm. "A phone interview is possible, isn't it?" she replied.

"Great idea," DeeDee said. "See what you can do, Brittany."

Brittany nodded, wishing they would go. She really didn't need all these hassles.

"Oh," DeeDee added, "and how about the interview with Tim and Nikki?"

"It's set up," Brittany said shortly. Half of it was, anyway. Nikki still hadn't gotten back to her about a good time for an interview. She would. Nikki was disgustingly reliable. "Now," Brittany said pointedly, "if you'll excuse me, I'm absolutely ravenous."

Leaving the lunch line, Brittany headed quickly for the table where Samantha and Kim were already sitting. If she had to answer one more question about the stupid newspaper, she'd scream.

How could she even think about her column when she had Jack on her mind? All of the night before she'd waited for him to call or come by, but the phone never rang, and neither did the doorbell.

When she got up in the morning, the first thing she started to do was call Jack. She stopped herself in the middle of dialing his number. If he really was angry, it was too soon to swallow her pride and beg for forgiveness. Maybe he wasn't mad. Maybe something had come up. Of course, he should have taken a minute to call her, but it had only been two days. Jack was as wild about her as she was about him. Wasn't he? If she waited a bit longer, he'd probably get lonely for her. As lonely as she was for him. It would be a lot easier to deal with all this if people would stop bugging her about unimportant details like columns and interviews.

"Well, well," Kim said the minute Brittany arrived at the lunch table. "This must be a record."

"What must be a record?" Brittany asked as she sat down.

"I saw you getting off the school bus this morning," Kim informed her. "That's the second day in a row Jack didn't drive you."

"So?" Brittany said coolly. Didn't Kim have anything better to do than keep tabs on her? "Jack doesn't drive me *every* day, you know. Like I said, he's very busy, and we just decided not to see so much of each other for a few days. It's no fun, but it won't last forever."

Samantha laughed. "I can just imagine the rapturous reunion you'll have," she said.

"So can I," Brittany agreed with a dreamy smile. Her friends went back to their food, and Brittany started to relax. They had no idea how miserable she was.

Her nerves started jangling again, though, when she spotted Jeremy Pratt watching her from across the crowded cafeteria. Raising one eyebrow, he shifted his glance to Kim, then back to Brittany.

Brittany gave him a microscopic nod. She might as well get to it, she thought.

"Speaking of romance," she said, "I've been hearing some very interesting things about Jeremy Pratt."

"Jeremy?" Samantha giggled. "The only thing he loves is his Porsche."

"Not quite," Brittany said. She looked pointedly at Kim. "From what I hear, he's desperately in love."

Kim narrowed her eyes. "Oh? Who with?"

Brittany didn't say a word.

"With *Kim?*" Samantha gasped.

"Ridiculous." Kim snorted, but a faint blush spread across her face.

Brittany smiled to herself. "Not so ridiculous," she said. "Remember when I sort of hinted to you at the country club dance that Jeremy might be the perfect guy for you?"

Kim nodded. "He asked me out twice," she said. "But—I don't know. He's good-looking, but I can't make up my mind about him."

"Well, he's made up his mind about you." Brittany leaned in closer to Kim. "I wasn't supposed to tell you this, but he was the one who asked me to talk to you about him."

"Really?" Kim's face turned a brighter shade of pink.

Brittany nodded.

"Why on earth didn't he speak for himself?" Samantha wanted to know.

Brittany shrugged. "Love does funny things to people, Samantha." She glanced swiftly at Jeremy. He was sitting alone for the moment, his chin in his hand, looking almost dreamy. Probably thinking up some other way to make my life miserable, she thought.

"Look at the guy," she said, nodding her head in his direction. "Is he in love or isn't he?"

"Hard to tell," Samantha decided.

Brittany wished Samantha would stop contradicting everything she said. "What do you think, Kim?"

Kim tore her eyes away from Jeremy. "I'm not sure. It's hard to believe, but he *could* be in love, I suppose. I think I'd need a little more evidence to be convinced, though."

Kim had tried to get the old crispness back into her voice, but she didn't quite succeed. She was definitely interested, Brittany could tell.

There. She'd set things in motion. With luck she'd soon have Jeremy Pratt off her back.

What next? Brittany groaned inwardly. The interview with Nikki and Tim, and the story about the Dead Beats.

Glancing around the cafeteria, she saw Nikki Masters sitting with her two best friends. The three of them looked extremely excited about something. Not long ago, Brittany was sure that one of that little clique was pregnant. She, Kim, and Samantha had had a lot of fun with that rumor, but it had all been a mistake. Still, Lacey looked ready to jump up and down. It must be something to do with her lumberjack-looking boyfriend, Brittany told herself.

But that thought immediately brought Jack to mind, and Brittany stopped wondering what Lacey was so happy about. She also lost interest in the interview with Nikki. She'd talk to Nikki another time. As for the Dead Beats, there was no way she could interview them, so why bother thinking about it?

Across the cafeteria Lacey was telling Nikki and Robin about her telephone conversation with the Dead Beats' manager. "I never thought it would be so easy!" she said excitedly.

"What did you do, anyway? Bribe the publicity manager?" Robin asked jokingly.

"I didn't need to," Lacey said with a laugh. "Anyway, I just told her it would be great for the Dead Beats' image if they went to a few smaller cities. Even if they couldn't do a concert, they could sign albums, shake hands, and prove they really appreciate *all* their fans." She took a sip of orange juice. "The woman agreed! She said they'd actually scheduled a session in another town, but they had to cancel because of plane connections. They're leaving Chicago next Saturday, and they'll make a stopover here, at noon. I nearly dropped the phone when she told me."

"Next Saturday, the Dead Beats are actually coming to River Heights," Nikki said dreamily.

"To Platters," Robin corrected her.

"Right," Lacey said. "Lenny was so ex-

cited he actually agreed to buy some advertising posters. Of course, somebody has to put
the posters up all over town. I'd do it, but
I've got student council meetings and work
and—'' She stopped talking and eyed her
friends.

"Uh-oh," Robin said. "I think we're about
to be enlisted, Nikki."

"I'll tell you what," Lacey offered. "If you
guys put the posters up, I'll drive both of you
to school for an entire week when I get my
car."

"Forget that," Robin told her with a grin.
"Just promise us a personal introduction to
the Dead Beats and we'll do anything you
want. Right, Nikki?"

Nikki nodded. "You bet."

Lacey burst into laughter. "It's a deal!"
she cried.

When her phone finally rang later that
night, Brittany grabbed for it like a drowning
person for a lifeline. "Jack?" she cried
breathlessly.

"Sorry to disappoint you," Kim said dryly. "Are you sure this separation period
between you and Jack is such a good idea,
Brittany? You sound desperate."

Brittany made a face at the phone. "Maybe
I do," she replied lightly. "But I'm probably

not half as desperate as Jack is." You *wish,* she added to herself.

"Well, anyway," Kim said. "Guess what?"

"What?" Brittany fluffed up her pillows and leaned back in bed.

"Jeremy Pratt sent me flowers," Kim said.

"No!" Brittany said.

"I don't believe it, either," Kim told her.

Brittany believed it. She'd sent the flowers herself after school while she was working at her mother's shop. It had been easy to put together a beautiful bouquet and stick it on the delivery truck. Her mother didn't know, of course, that Brittany had paid for it out of her own money. It wasn't easy to part with fifteen dollars, but it would be worth it to get Jeremy Pratt off her back.

"Well?" she asked. "Are they pretty?"

"Oh, sort of," Kim said. "If you like daisies. I prefer roses, actually."

Brittany gritted her teeth. Jeremy was rich enough to send roses, but *she* certainly wasn't. Besides, it wasn't as though Kim got flowers every day of her life.

"But I suppose that's not the point," Kim said.

"I agree."

"And the card's not bad at all."

"Oh?" Brittany had thought long and hard over that card.

"'Like flowers in a garden,'" Kim quoted, "'you bloom in my heart.' Who'd have thought Jeremy was so romantic?"

Nobody, Brittany wanted to say. "That's really exciting, don't you think?" she asked. "If I were you, I'd be melting."

"Well, you're not me," Kim pointed out. "But—"

"But?"

"If he asks me again, I'll go out with him," Kim announced.

They chatted for a few more minutes. Then as soon as Brittany hung up, she found Jeremy's phone number and called him.

"It's Brittany," she said as soon as he answered. "Ask Kim out fast, before she changes her mind."

Without waiting for Jeremy's response, Brittany hung up, breathing a sigh of relief. She'd kept her part of the bargain, and the whole unpleasant business was over and done with.

Leaning back on the pillows again, Brittany picked up her French book and tried to study. But it was hopeless. She had to straighten out her irregular life before she could deal with irregular verbs.

With another sigh, Brittany sat up and slid her feet into her purple satin slippers. It was time for a diet soda.

She was almost to the bedroom door when

the phone rang again. Probably Kim, wanting to tell her that Jeremy had called. She picked up the receiver. "Hello?"

"Hi, Brittany," a deep male voice said softly. "I had to call you. I haven't been able to get you out of my mind."

# 6 ～～～

It wasn't Jack.

Brittany felt a sharp disappointment. "Who is this?" she asked. "Is this a joke?"

"No joke, I promise," he said.

"Then why don't you tell me who you are?" she said.

"Can't you tell?" the voice asked. "I'll give you a hint—our score was love."

Dustin Tucker. The blond tennis instructor. Brittany didn't have any trouble at all picturing his face—brown-eyed, tanned, ruggedly handsome. Well, well, she thought with a smile. "Hi, Dustin," she said casually. "This is a surprise."

"Is it?" Dustin chuckled. "After that game on Sunday, I thought you might have been expecting me to call."

Of course, Brittany thought. Why should she be surprised? After all, she'd pulled out all the stops flirting with him. How was he to know it was just an act?

"Well," she said, smiling into the phone, "I suppose I did think there'd be a chance of hearing from you. We might not have won the game, but we made quite a team." This was fun. This was exactly what she needed to take her mind off other, more unpleasant matters.

"Good. I'm glad we see eye to eye on that," Dustin said. "So. How about getting together?"

A date? This would take a bit of thinking. "Dustin?" Brittany said sweetly. "Would you mind holding on a moment?" She put the receiver down on the bed and frowned at the opposite wall.

Did she really want to go out with Dustin Tucker? He was certainly gorgeous enough; she wouldn't even consider it otherwise. He wasn't Jack Reilly, though.

Jack hadn't called her for two days. Why should she sit around moping and worrying when she could be out having fun?

But what if Jack heard about it? Dustin was at the club every day. Jack was bound to run into him there.

Maybe if Jack heard she'd been stealing a

few kisses from somebody else, he just might remember what he'd been missing. He'd probably be so jealous that he'd stop being mad and start wishing he'd never made such a big deal about a little harmless flirting. Then he'd call her to make up, and the two of them would be right back where they'd started.

Brittany picked up the phone. "Dustin? I'd love to get together. The sooner the better."

"Are you out of your mind?" Samantha asked the next day during sit-ups in gym class. Her breath hissed out as she flopped down on her back. "I don't mind telling you, Brittany, you're playing with fire."

Hands behind her head, Brittany sat up and touched her elbows to her knees. "Playing with fire is exciting, Samantha—as long as you don't get burned."

"Well, of course," Samantha agreed. "But I'm really curious about how you're going to go through with this without getting at least a tiny bit scorched."

The gym teacher blew her whistle and switched the class to jumping jacks.

Hopping up and down, her arms swinging, Brittany gasped, "Jack doesn't need to know about this date. And if he finds out, I'll persuade him that *he's* the one I really care about."

"I know, you're very persuasive," Samantha puffed. "But, Brittany, why? I mean Jack's *gorgeous!* And he's in college, and he's really nice. What do you need Dustin for?"

The whistle blew again. "Hit the showers, ladies!" the gym teacher yelled.

"Finally," Brittany gasped gratefully.

"You didn't answer my question," Samantha reminded her as they headed into the locker room. "Why bother dating Dustin when you've got Jack?"

For a second Brittany was tempted to confide the truth: that she wasn't sure she *did* have Jack.

But the temptation passed quickly. Samantha might promise not to tell anyone, but sooner or later she'd slip and mention it. Then the rumor would be all over River Heights High like the plague.

"Well?" Samantha asked.

Stepping out of her gym suit, Brittany wrapped herself in a fluffy white towel and gave Samantha what she hoped was a pitying look. "Don't you know, Samantha?" she asked. "It's never a good idea to let yourself be taken for granted."

Before Samantha could ask any more bothersome questions, Brittany entered the shower and turned on the water. Gym was her last class. Usually she hated showering in the locker room, but that day she didn't mind. After school she'd have to work at Blooms, and Dustin was picking her up at home right after that. She'd barely have time to change clothes, let alone shower.

Dinner, Dustin had said. Standing under the skimpy spray, Brittany wondered what it would be like. Candlelight at the country club? Or something a little more casual, like that new restaurant with the band and the flashing lights?

Whatever it turned out to be, Brittany was starting to look forward to the date. She'd almost convinced herself that it was the best thing that could have happened. Maybe Jack *was* taking her for granted. Well, this would show him.

A few minutes later, dried and dressed, Brittany was hurrying to her locker when she spotted Karen Jacobs and DeeDee Smith at the far end of the hall. They hadn't seen her yet.

Quickly Brittany ducked around the corner and bent over the water fountain. She couldn't make out much of what DeeDee was saying as they passed, but she did catch the words *Dead Beats*.

Great, she thought, gulping water. They're probably wondering why I haven't arranged an exclusive interview. She knew she should have called the Dead Beats' manager. She would, just as soon as she got things straightened out with Jack. She'd get the interview, and DeeDee would forget that the whole idea had been Karen's. Brittany's job as next year's editor would be practically guaranteed.

Taking one last drink, Brittany saw a pair of slim buttery-leather boots out of the corner of her eye. She'd seen those boots at the mall the other day—more than twenty allowances. Kim, of course.

Straightening up, she noticed that Kim's face didn't have its usual bored expression. In fact, she looked slightly nervous and her cheeks were flushed.

"Are you sick?" Brittany asked. "Your eyes are all glittery."

"Thanks a lot," Kim said. "No, I'm not sick. I'm excited."

"Oh? Oh!" Brittany remembered. "You mean Jeremy followed up those flowers with an invitation?" He'd better have. She wasn't about to spend any more money on this.

Kim nodded. "We're going out tonight."

Brittany hoped she and Dustin didn't run into them. Kim wasn't as easy to fool as

Samantha. "That's great," she said. "I'm sure you two will hit it off. You have so much in common."

"Well, to tell you the truth, I'm a little worried," Kim admitted. "I don't really know Jeremy at all. I hope we find something to talk about."

How about the size of Jeremy's trust fund? Brittany wanted to say. Instead she laughed. "Well, take my advice and don't talk *too* much. The silences are fun, too, if you know what I mean."

"This is a first date, Brittany," Kim pointed out. To Brittany's surprise, Kim's face got pinker and her eyes got brighter.

So, Brittany thought, amused. Kim was actually nervous. Well, she'd better warn Jeremy. If he fell all over her, Kim would probably blame Brittany.

"Of course," Brittany agreed. "I wasn't talking about anything ultra-serious. I'm sure Jeremy's a perfect gentleman."

Five minutes later she spotted Jeremy, the perfect snake, heading for his car. Brittany was hurrying to catch the bus for the mall, so she didn't go into detail. She just grabbed Jeremy by the arm of his expensive hand-knit sweater and said, "Don't come on too strong with Kim tonight."

Jeremy was too surprised to say anything.

"That was inside information I just gave

you," Brittany added over her shoulder as she hurried away. "Now you owe *me* a favor, Jeremy."

Later, Brittany stood at the door of her bedroom closet, trying to decide what to wear. The worst thing about working at the mall was walking by all those store windows and seeing all the gorgeous clothes. But she could hardly buy a new outfit every other day of the week.

Of course, anything in her wardrobe would be new to Dustin. If only she knew where he was taking her, it would make her decision a lot easier. But she didn't know his phone number, and besides, he'd be there in fifteen minutes.

"Where are you going?"

Brittany turned and glared at Tamara, who was standing in the doorway, an apple in her hand. "Don't you ever knock?" she asked acidly.

"I did. Don't you ever hear?" Tamara retorted.

"Out," Brittany ordered. "I'm in a hurry."

Tamara took a bite of apple and shifted her weight to the other foot. "Is Jack taking you out?" she asked.

Brittany pulled out her black leather miniskirt. "Mind your own business."

"I think you two had a fight," Tamara

went on. "What did you do to make him mad?"

"What makes you think *I* did something?" Brittany slipped on a red silk blouse.

Tamara grinned. "Come on, Brittany. This is your sister you're talking to. I live in the same house with you, remember? I *know* you."

"Not as well as you think you do," Brittany informed her. "Jack and I did not have a fight." She put on a black silky vest with red and yellow flowers, shut the closet door, and headed for her bureau.

"So who are you going out with?" Tamara persisted.

"I just said we didn't have a fight!" Brittany practically screamed.

"I know," Tamara said calmly. "But Jack never takes you out on Wednesday. That's his history seminar night. And, anyway, don't you have homework?"

Brittany sighed. "His name's Dustin Tucker. He's a tennis instructor at the club. He'll be here in seven minutes. I told him I had to be back by nine, and that's when I'll do my homework. Now will you go away and let me get my makeup on?"

Tamara finally moved toward the hall. "Well," she called back over her shoulder, "I think you're crazy. Nobody could be as great as Jack."

Brittany was tempted to throw the hairbrush at her. Of course Dustin couldn't compare to Jack, but that didn't mean he wasn't special in his own way.

Taking a deep breath to calm herself, Brittany studied her face in the mirror and then went to work. Lipstick, of course, but not too much. A little more blusher than usual. Her summer tan was long gone, and she didn't want to appear pale next to Dustin. Finally, she bent forward and brushed her silky dark hair, then flung it back, letting it tumble into waves around her shoulders.

Perfect. Very natural looking. But with the outfit, pretty sophisticated, too. A combination that never failed with guys. And she'd done it with two minutes to spare.

# 7

Twenty minutes later Brittany was sitting on the edge of her bed, one foot swinging impatiently. Five minutes late was acceptable, but twenty was an insult. Where was he? Had she possibly gotten the day wrong?

That was when she heard what sounded like a putt-putt car at a carnival. Brittany crossed the room, pulled back the curtain, and peered through her bedroom window. Under the yellow glow of the streetlight, a battered, rusty, VW bug chugged to a halt in front of the house. A fuzzy red flower drooped from the top of its antenna.

Quickly, Brittany dropped the curtain. It's not Dustin, she told herself. It's somebody who's looking for a junkyard and got lost.

The doorbell rang. Brittany waited. Then Tamara screeched, "Brittany! Your date's here!"

Brittany picked up her jacket and small black purse with the long gold chain. Oh, well, she thought as she left the room. VW bugs are practically collectors' items.

When Brittany got to the front door, her parents were there, chatting with Dustin. Well, chatting wasn't exactly the right word. They were being polite.

"Brittany," Mr. Tate said when he saw her. "There you are. My, don't you look nice."

"Sure do," Dustin agreed.

"Thank you." Brittany smiled brightly and moved toward the door, but her mother put a hand on her arm.

"Honey," Mrs. Tate said, "could I see you in the kitchen for just a minute?"

Here it comes, Brittany thought. Sure enough, when she and her mother got into the kitchen, Mrs. Tate said, "Sweetie, when I agreed to let you go out for dinner on a school night, I assumed it was with Jack."

"I'll still be home by nine, Mom, I promise. And I don't have very much homework," Brittany said. "You don't have to worry about Dustin, either. He's a nice guy. Jack knows him."

"Well, that's good to hear," Mrs. Tate said. She smoothed a stray hair back from Brittany's face. "You certainly have the right to choose your dates, but—well, I hope nothing's wrong between you and Jack. Your father and I like him so much."

So do I, Brittany thought. "Jack's awfully busy right now," she said. "Anyway, one dinner with Dustin doesn't mean I'm breaking up with Jack."

Her mother still looked a little worried, but she didn't say anything else. She and Brittany rejoined Dustin and Mr. Tate, who looked relieved to see them. They probably couldn't find a thing to talk about, Brittany thought. She was sure Dustin and her father had nothing in common. She started to remember how well Jack and her father got along and then stopped herself. This date was with Dustin. She had to forget about Jack Reilly for the time being.

Mr. Tate kissed her on the forehead. "Well, honey, have a good time." He gave Brittany a questioning look, and she knew he was dying to ask about Jack, too.

Dustin assured him he'd have Brittany back on time, and they said goodbye and walked out to his car.

A collector's item it wasn't. It was exactly what it appeared to be: a perfect candidate for the junkyard.

Hiding her distaste, Brittany slid into the front seat and immediately snagged her stockings on a piece of metal poking through the seat cover. He must have borrowed the car, she decided. *His* is probably in the shop.

When Dustin got in, he reached across the gearshift and squeezed her hand. "You look fantastic, did I tell you that?"

"Yes, but I don't mind hearing it again," she said. "You don't look bad yourself."

Actually, he didn't look all *that* great. Jeans, a plain white shirt, and a gray sweatshirt. What did he have planned for dinner, anyway? Burgers and fries?

Dustin started the car and it lurched forward. A symphony of rattles and clanks started up from the tiny space behind the front seats.

"Soda," Dustin said, seeing the look on her face. "Got at least thirty cans of it back there. I hope it's enough."

Brittany cleared her throat. "Enough for what?"

"Didn't I tell you?"

"No, you didn't." Brittany had the feeling she wasn't going to like this.

"I thought I did," he said. "Well, some friends of mine are having a cookout over at Moon Lake. That's where we're going."

A picnic! No wonder he was dressed so casually, Brittany thought. The least he could have done was remember to tell her. "Dustin," she said, trying not to sound too annoyed, "I think I should go back and change. I'm not really dressed for a picnic."

"Don't worry about it," he said, squeezing her hand again. "You have to be home by nine, and if we go back now, we'll lose a lot of time." He shrugged. "You're a little over-dressed, but you'll be the best-looking girl there."

As Dustin and Brittany chugged toward the lake, Jeremy Pratt nosed his Porsche into a parking space at the country club.

"Well," he said, turning to smile at Kim. "Here we are."

"Yes," Kim agreed. It wasn't a clever answer, but she was nervous.

"I don't usually eat so early," Jeremy said as they walked toward the clubhouse. "But since we have school tomorrow, I thought it would be better."

"Oh, that's all right," Kim told him. Actually, she was wondering if Jeremy would take her hand while they walked, but he didn't.

It was strange, she'd never given Jeremy Pratt much thought, not even after the first time Brittany had spoken to her about him. True, he was rich and good-looking. He was also a snob, but Kim didn't hold that against him. Maybe it was because she'd known him forever. It was hard to think romantically about somebody who'd been your deskmate in kindergarten.

But when Brittany had hinted that Jeremy was in love, and then he'd actually sent the flowers and that note, Kim had reconsidered. If Jeremy really *was* in love with her, life would be very interesting. She didn't love him, of course, but that didn't matter. She could always pretend. If he loved her, then he'd belong to her. She liked the idea of having that kind of power, especially over someone like Jeremy Pratt.

Still, the whole love idea was intriguing. What would it feel like to be kissed by somebody who was in love with you? Stealing a glance at Jeremy's chiseled profile, Kim felt a shiver run up her spine. She couldn't wait to find out.

Brittany slogged her way toward the lake. Jagged rocks and wet sand kept tripping her up, and she knew her suede boots would be beyond repair before the night was over.

Every time she stumbled, Dustin grabbed her hand and said, "Whoa!" It reminded her of the way people talked to horses. She wished she had a horse, in fact. She'd get to the campfire a lot faster, and with dry feet.

Not that she really wanted to get there. A

cookout at the lake was hardly her idea of a romantic dinner. Not even the moon climbing in the sky could make this outing romantic. Soda and hot dogs, she thought with a sigh. She detested hot dogs. And she was dressed completely wrong. Everybody would stare at her. Being the center of attention was one thing, but being a laughingstock was entirely different.

"It's too bad you forgot to tell me this was what we'd be doing," Brittany said again. "I'm afraid I won't be able to join in any beach games dressed like this."

Hint, hint. Maybe Dustin would suggest they go somewhere else. Anywhere that had tables and chairs and a solid floor.

Chuckling, Dustin reached for her hand as she stumbled again. "Don't worry about that," he said. "Some of the guys might want to get up a game of volleyball. But the only beach games I plan on playing are with you."

Brittany's spirits took a turn for the better. This was more like it. Dustin's hand was strong and warm, and he was obviously extremely interested. She supposed she could stand one evening in the great outdoors.

The dining room at the River Heights Country Club had several secluded spots where small tables for two were tucked away behind pillars and screens. But Jeremy had requested a table smack in the middle of the large, brightly lit main hall. Much safer, he thought, remembering Brittany's warning. Now Kim wouldn't worry about him making a move on her.

Not that he'd planned on making a move. It was much too soon for that. Kim Bishop was extremely particular when it came to boys, and Jeremy wasn't about to do anything to turn her off.

He and Kim were a perfect match, he thought, unfolding his snow white linen napkin. Together, Jeremy Pratt and Kim Bishop would be invincible. They'd rule the River Heights High social scene in style. Jeremy knew he couldn't do it on his own. He needed a girl, and Kim was the obvious choice. All he had to do was be his usual smooth self. The moves could come later.

He'd have to kiss her eventually, Jeremy realized. Not that night, of course, but sometime. Now, watching Kim bite into a cheese straw, he decided it wouldn't be difficult. With her smooth blond hair and clear blue eyes, she was quite beautiful.

Kim's looks were a bonus. This was a political match, but Jeremy decided it could definitely turn out to be something more.

\*　\*　\*

This is a horrible dream, Brittany decided. There is no sand in my boots, and I'm not sitting on a slippery, moss-covered log. In a minute I'll wake up and this entire lakeside fiasco will disappear.

There was a thump at her feet and a fresh spray of sand flew up, sprinkling her skirt. Brittany looked down at the white volleyball and had to admit that her nightmare was real. She wasn't asleep at all.

"Hey, Brit!" one of Dustin's friends shouted. "Toss it back over here!"

I'd rather toss it in the lake, Brittany thought grimly. Easing herself off the log, she picked up the filthy ball and heaved it back.

"Thanks, Brit!"

Brit. She hated that nickname. It was even worse than Britty, which was what Tamara called her sometimes.

It wasn't that Dustin's friends were awful. They were all about his age, and they seemed nice enough. But so far all they'd done was stuff themselves and then play ball. Even the two other girls—who were wearing jeans, naturally—didn't have much to say.

Thank goodness Dustin wasn't like them. Right now he was over by the campfire, roasting a hot dog, but he'd been as good as his word and stuck by her the whole time. So far, he hadn't kissed her, but Brittany knew it was inevitable. His dark brown eyes gleamed hungrily whenever he looked at her.

"Hey, Brittany," Dustin said, trotting back with a hot dog in each hand. "What do you say we take a little walk along the shore?" He smiled down at her. "The moon's up now, and it's beautiful."

Brittany stood up and tucked her hand through his arm. "I can't think of anything I'd rather do," she told him in a silky voice.

The kiss was coming up, she could tell. She might just make it through this horrible evening after all.

Frowning, Kim put down her fork and reached for her water glass. She wished she had some aspirin. The bright lights were giving her a headache. Why had Jeremy picked this table, anyway? There were older people sitting all around them. They couldn't even hold hands without feeling as if they were onstage.

So far, though, Jeremy hadn't touched her, not even by accident when he handed her the bread basket. Instead, he'd kept up a running monologue about school, the club, his family, and *her* family. Not only was Kim bored, she was disappointed. When was he going to get to the good stuff?

Taking another sip of water, Kim sneaked

a look at Jeremy over the rim of the glass. He was staring at his dish of chocolate mousse, not talking for once. Before he had a chance to start up again, Kim decided to get things rolling.

Clearing her throat, she tried to make her voice sound husky and inviting. "By the way, Jeremy, I don't think I thanked you for the flowers you sent. They were beautiful. And so was the note."

Jeremy raised his eyes and she waited for him to smile. Instead he frowned.

"Flowers?" he asked blankly.

"Yes," she said. "Daisies."

Jeremy shook his head and laughed. "Kim, I don't send daisies. I send long-stemmed roses."

"Oh? What's the matter, don't you think I'm good enough for roses?"

"I didn't say that," he protested. "What I'm saying is I didn't send you any flowers." It wouldn't have been a bad idea, though.

"Well, somebody did," Kim told him. "They came from Blooms and there was this very romantic note—" She broke off and stared at him. "Brittany did it!" she cried. "That sneak!"

Jeremy suddenly realized what had happened, but it was too late to take back what he'd said. "Listen, maybe she did, but she was probably just trying to help me—"

"Oh, so it was a setup?" Kim snapped angrily. "What did you two have planned, anyway? Some big joke? Make Kim think Jeremy's in love with her and then have a good laugh?"

"In love?" Jeremy's face went pale. "Who said anything about love?"

"You did! I mean, Brittany did, in the note!" Kim stood up quickly, glaring at him. "Well, let me tell you something, Jeremy Pratt. I wouldn't fall in love with you if you were the last guy on earth! I've sat here with you for an hour and a half and guess what? You're about as exciting as that trout you ate for dinner!" She took a deep breath. "Don't bother driving me home. I'll call a taxi."

Jeremy was on his feet now, too. "Kim, listen," he said. "I asked Brittany to talk to you about going out with me. I never asked her to send flowers and love notes. If you want to be mad at somebody, be mad at her!"

"Don't worry, I am," Kim told him. "In fact, the next time I see her, I just might kill her!"

With that, Kim strode out of the dining room, leaving Jeremy alone, the center of attention. Sheepishly motioning for the check, he signed for it and walked out.

What a disaster! His chances with Kim were completely nil, thanks to Brittany. He didn't blame Kim for being furious. He was furious, too. He'd do much worse than kill Brittany. He'd *ruin* her. It wouldn't be long before Brittany Tate was finished at River Heights High.

Brittany had to admit that the moonlight on the lake *was* beautiful. It was too bad she wasn't seeing it from a comfortable car, with the heater running full blast.

"Cold?" Without waiting for an answer, Dustin put his arm around her and pulled her to him.

"Mmm," Brittany murmured. She waited for the familiar tingling to start up. Maybe it did, but she couldn't tell the difference between it and the shivers she kept getting.

Dustin dropped his second hot dog in the sand and put his other arm around her. Now they were face-to-face.

Brittany smiled up at him. Her lips were numb but ready to meet his. He kissed her finally, softly at first. She waited again for the sparks to fly, but finally she realized they weren't going to.

Dustin was gorgeous. He just wasn't Jack.

# 8

"Well, Lacey," Mr. Dupree said at breakfast the next morning. "How's your promotion for the rock group coming along?"

Lacey gulped down some orange juice and smiled. "It's going fine," she said. "So far, anyway. I thought the hardest part would be getting the Dead Beats to agree to come. But that was pretty easy. It's the details that are tricky — getting the posters done, taking out ads, hiring a limo to pick up the group at the airport."

"I have to admit, I had my doubts about all of this, but you seem to be handling things very well," Lacey's mother said approvingly.

"We're proud of you," Mr. Dupree added, picking up his briefcase.

"Thanks," Lacey said. "When I finally get my car, I'll know I really earned it. Maybe you and Mom have been right all along." Taking a last drink of juice, Lacey hurried outside with her father, who was giving her a lift to school. She just knew that her hard work on this promotion would pay off—big time.

"The posters will be ready tomorrow," Lacey announced to Robin and Nikki when she joined them on the quad. "You can put them up over the weekend, okay?"

"We'll be ready," Nikki assured her.

"Count on it," Robin agreed. Then she laughed. "I think you've found your calling, Lacey—organizing tours of rock groups."

"Don't tell that to Rick," Lacey warned. "He's already complaining that we don't see enough of each other. Things haven't even started hopping yet. Wait till next week." She grinned. "After next Saturday, it'll be back to the same old grind."

"No, it won't," Nikki said. "You'll be earning more money, remember?"

"Right!" Lacey said. "It's all been so much fun, though. The posters and ordering the records from Chicago and getting ads in the papers and—oh!" She clapped a hand to her forehead. "I almost forgot! I've got to get hold of DeeDee Smith and make sure she gets the ad in next week's *Record*. Talk to you later!''

Robin looked after her, shaking her head. "I think Lacey *has* found her calling. Uh, Nikki?"

"Don't move," Nikki said softly. "I'm standing behind you."

Robin looked puzzled. "Are you going to tell me why, or do I have to guess?"

"Brittany's heading this way," Nikki said. "I don't want her to see me. She's been bugging me to give her an interview, remember? I'm hoping she'll forget about it."

"Oh, sure," Robin said dryly. "Come on, Nikki. You have one of the lead roles. You've got to expect the *Record* to do a piece about you."

"About the play," Nikki corrected her. "Not about me."

Robin understood. Nikki had had her fill of newspaper stories written about her. And Robin didn't trust Brittany Tate—the girl would probably bring up the murder in her article just to make Nikki squirm.

"You can relax now," Robin told Nikki after Brittany had passed them. "The shark has gone in search of another kill."

But Nikki Masters was the last thing on Brittany's mind at that moment. She'd spent the bus ride to school thinking about her date with Dustin. It had been awful, but she *had* enjoyed being with Dustin. He wasn't Jack, though. She refused to think about Jack right then. If she did, she might really start to panic. She hadn't heard from Jack since Sunday.

Across the quad, Brittany caught sight of Kim and Samantha. They were on the front steps in a crowd of kids, waiting until the last minute to go inside. Brittany picked up her pace, eager to find out if Kim's date had turned out any better than hers.

Kim and Samantha had their heads together, and Kim's mouth was going a mile a minute. Then Samantha put her hand on Kim's arm and nodded toward Brittany.

Kim gazed out across the quad and folded her arms. Even from a distance, Brittany could tell that her friend was furious.

What could possibly be the matter with Kim? *She* probably had the kind of date Brittany had been hoping for.

As Brittany approached, Kim's eyes narrowed until they were practically slits.

Brittany stopped. "Kim?" she said. "What's going on?"

Kim held up a hand and everyone around her got very quiet. In a loud, clear voice, she said, "I'm going to tell you this one time, Brittany Tate. Then I don't want anything more to do with you." She paused dramatically. "You're a liar and a sneak. Our friendship—ha, ha—is over."

With that, she turned around and stalked into the building.

There was a moment of stunned silence. Brittany stood alone, her mouth hanging open, but when she heard the buzz of excited conversation start up, she quickly snapped it shut.

By noon the entire school knew that Kim Bishop and Brittany Tate were no longer friends. No one knew exactly why, though. Kim hadn't told anyone except Samantha, and Brittany certainly wasn't about to start explaining.

"I didn't lie," she insisted to Samantha. "I only hinted."

They were sitting at a cafeteria table together. Fortunately for Brittany, Kim hadn't come to lunch that day.

Samantha sighed. "All I know is, Kim said that Jeremy Pratt's a loathsome skunk, that it was the most horrible date she'd ever been on, and that you had made a fool out of her." She sighed again. "I think that last part was the worst for her. You know how proud she is."

"I refuse to feel guilty," Brittany declared. "Okay, so I stretched the truth a little when I said Jeremy might be in love with her," she admitted. "So what? He must be interested, at least. Why else would he want to date her?"

"Who knows why Jeremy Pratt would want to do anything?" Samantha said with a shrug.

"At least Kim was right about one thing," Brittany remarked acidly. "He *is* a loathsome skunk." She remembered how Jeremy had blackmailed her into setting up this date. She couldn't tell that part to Samantha, of course, but she planned to have a little chat about it with Mr. Pratt. If anyone should feel guilty, he should.

Having Kim mad at her was bad enough, but to have the entire school talking about it was almost more than Brittany could bear. Just the memory of that awful, silent moment after Kim had yelled at her was enough to make her want to run and hide.

Brittany had her pride, though. She would face this, no matter how painful it might be.

Besides, she told herself, she had plenty of other friends. She hadn't made herself the center of so many clubs and organizations for nothing. Kim would come around eventually. Until then, Brittany would do just fine without her.

First things first, though. She had to find Jeremy Pratt. He'd tell her exactly what had

happened the night before. Then she'd wring
his neck.

"We can't talk here, Brittany," Jeremy
said when she finally cornered him in the
hall later that day. He practically shoved
Brittany through the doorway of an empty
classroom.

Brittany glared at him. "Why can't we talk
in the hall?"

"Simple," Jeremy said with a shrug. "I
don't want Kim to see us together. I haven't
given up on her yet, but if she sees me with
you, she'll never give me a second chance."

"Well, don't blame *me* if you had a lousy
date," Brittany snapped. "Exactly what did
you do to Kim to make her so mad? She's
ready to kill me, you know."

Jeremy sighed and looked at the ceiling.
"Brittany, I did nothing but follow your
advice."

"What advice? I didn't give you any advice."

"Sure you did," he said. "I quote: 'Don't
come on too strong with Kim.'"

Brittany shrugged. "So?"

"So it was bad advice. I think Kim was
expecting a little romance, maybe even a kiss
or two." Jeremy looked at Brittany angrily.
"I can't say that I blame her, after those

flowers I supposedly sent. Not to mention the romantic note that went with them."

The stupid daisies! She'd forgotten to tell him. Brittany groaned inwardly.

"All right, maybe I shouldn't have sent them," she admitted. "But they got you the date with Kim, didn't they? What else did you expect—a guarantee? 'Have a wonderful time or double your money back'?"

"Don't you get it?" Jeremy gave her an icy stare. "I wanted a date, that's it. Nice and simple. But, no, you had to mess everything up for me."

"Well, next time get your own date," Brittany said angrily.

"I will. If there is a next time," Jeremy told her.

The bell rang then, and Jeremy started toward the door. Then he turned and gave Brittany a cool smile. "By the way, don't be surprised if nobody else wants to be seen with you, either, Brittany," he said. "I get the feeling that Kim's ruining you around here, and I'm with her all the way."

And I was going to wring his neck, Brittany thought in frustration. Somehow, Jeremy Pratt had turned the tables on her. She didn't like that one bit.

Lips pressed tightly together, Brittany flounced out of the room and stormed down the hall to her next class. She'd figure out a way to deal with Jeremy and Kim. She just had to keep cool until then. A tiny shiver of fear ran up her spine. "Kim's out to ruin you." Of course, Brittany was more popular in general, but Kim did have a lot of influence. And if Jeremy Pratt was on her case, too, life could get very unpleasant.

"Brittany?"

"What?" Brittany almost screeched. Whirling around, she found herself face-to-face with Karen Jacobs.

With an effort, she put on a tiny smile. "Oh. Hi, Karen." She turned and kept walking, but Karen matched her, step for step. What did this annoying girl want, anyway?

"DeeDee asked me to mention that column you wrote," Karen said. "The one on the Dead Beats."

"Oh?" Now Karen was DeeDee's messenger, Brittany thought contemptuously. "What about it?" She'd written the article quickly last night and turned it in that morning, so it was possible she could have messed up.

"The story was okay," Karen said slowly. "It's just that Lacey Dupree was in this morning, putting in an ad for that record store she works in."

"Mmm." Brittany was barely listening.

"Well, Lacey got the Dead Beats to agree to an autographing session in the store."

Brittany was stunned. The Dead Beats were coming to Platters? How on earth had Lacey managed that?

Still, she didn't want Karen to guess that she was completely clueless about the whole thing. "Oh, right. I was going to tell DeeDee that myself," she lied.

"You mean you knew about it?" Karen asked.

"Well, sure." Brittany shrugged.

Karen brightened. "Pretty exciting, huh?"

Brittany agreed that having the Dead Beats in town would be fantastic, but secretly she was extremely annoyed. Somehow, the Mouse had done the impossible. And DeeDee was sure to point out that fact.

"Well, anyway," Karen went on, "DeeDee said you can do next week's column on whatever you want, since the Dead Beats aren't coming till next Saturday. But she'd like you to get an interview with them for the issue after that."

"That's exactly what I was planning to do," Brittany told her.

"Okay," Karen said. "I'm also supposed to remind you about that article about Tim and Nikki."

Brittany felt like exploding, but she kept her voice level. "Why didn't DeeDee remind me herself?"

Karen stopped walking and shrugged, her hazel eyes matching the pale green of her sweater. "I don't know. Maybe because you're never in the *Record* office anymore," she said. "Listen, Brittany, I've got to go. I'll see you later, okay?"

Fuming, Brittany watched the girl walk away. She was sure of it now — Karen Jacobs was out to get the editor-in-chief's job next year. She acted so sweet and helpful, but she was obviously trying to score points with DeeDee. Her little remark about Brittany's not being around enough had given her away.

Brittany sighed. First Kim, then Jeremy. Now Karen Jacobs. She couldn't handle all this at once. Glancing at her watch as she hurried on down the hall, she saw that there was an hour and a half left till school was over. Could she possibly make it through the rest of this horrible day without blowing up?

By the time the last bell rang, Brittany's nerves were shot. Nothing else terrible had happened, but that was hardly anything to cheer about.

She hadn't been able to concentrate on her last two classes at all. Kim's scathing words, Jeremy's threat, Karen's sneaky hint that she wasn't pulling her weight on the paper — the whole mess kept whirling in her mind.

For practically the first time in living

memory, Brittany didn't stop to do a quick makeup check at her locker before leaving the building. Instead, she bypassed her locker completely and headed straight outside. She didn't have to go to work, thank goodness. She could go right home, be completely miserable, and think of ways to fight back.

Once outside, though, Brittany changed her mind about going home. Or rather, the battered and rusty VW made her change it. Dustin was waiting for her.

He was smiling at Brittany, his teeth very white against his tanned face. He gave her a lazy wave.

She could come up with a battle plan later, Brittany thought, sailing down the steps toward the car. Right now, she wanted to forget about this horrible day. And Dustin Tucker was just the person to help her do it.

# 9

"Really, Brittany, sometimes you're a true mystery," Samantha drawled over the phone Sunday night. "I mean, just how long do you plan to go out with this Dustin guy?"

Brittany was reclining on her bed. "You're not interested in him, are you?"

Samantha laughed lightly. "Well, I might have been, but I'd never dream of intruding on your territory."

"I didn't think so."

"Well, anyway, Brittany, tell me the truth," Samantha said. "Is Jack really too busy to see you right now?"

"Of course!" Brittany sounded very indignant.

"Then why settle for Dustin when you'll

have the real thing back in your arms soon?"
Samantha asked.

Easy for *you* to say, Brittany thought.
She had no idea how long it might be before she and Jack got together again. *If* they
ever did. "Well, I hate sitting at home," she
said.

Samantha laughed again. "Well, you sure
haven't been doing that! I tried to call you
five times this weekend and you were either
out or on your way out. So where did Dustin
take you?"

"Oh, here and there," Brittany replied
vaguely, hoping Samantha wouldn't pump
her for details. Dustin was definitely not a
big spender. They'd gone out for pizza once,
and earlier that day he'd brought along sub-
marine sandwiches that they ate at a table by
the lake.

Dustin didn't exactly live up to her romantic standards, either. Kissing him was nice
enough, but her heart didn't pound the way it
did with Jack.

Still, he *was* extremely good looking and
an older guy. He was enough for now. Actually, he was *all* for now. It had been a week
since Brittany had heard anything from
Jack. She'd reached for the phone to call him
so many times, but she told herself to hang
on just a little bit longer. How much longer
could she wait? Every time Brittany thought

about Jack, she had to force herself not to cry.

"Anyway," she said to Samantha, "why did you call me so much? Did something happen?"

Samantha hesitated. "No, nothing much. Except—well, I talked to Kim."

Brittany's hand tightened on the phone, but she kept her voice light. "Oh? Has she decided to let me live?"

"I'm not sure." Samantha sighed. "I tried to discuss the whole thing with her, but she refused to let me mention your name, even."

"I'm not surprised," Brittany said. "She can be pretty stubborn, but if she thinks I'm going to beg for her forgiveness, she can think again."

"Well, just watch yourself," Samantha said in a warning tone. "Kim could set a world record for the longest grudge ever held. And she can make life very unpleasant for the grudgee."

"Stop the car!" Lacey shrieked.

Rick Stratton stepped so hard on the brake that their seat belts locked. "What?" he asked, looking around wildly. "A cat? A dog? I didn't see anything!"

It was Monday morning, and Rick was driving Lacey to school. "What was it?" he asked again, his eyes searching the street.

"Not there!" Lacey cried. *"There!"*

Rick followed her finger to where she was pointing—at the side of a building—and saw one of the posters advertising the Dead Beats' arrival in River Heights.

He sighed in relief, but he was obviously annoyed, too. "Come on, Lacey. I thought I was about to run over something."

"I know, I'm sorry, but *look!*" She sounded frantic. "Look at the date!"

" 'The seventeenth,' " he read aloud. "I don't get it."

"The seventeenth is Friday," Lacey said. "But they're coming on *Saturday!*"

Rick whistled. "Now I get it," he said.

"I just don't believe it," Lacey fumed as they drove on. "I went to the printer personally. I wrote the thing out myself. I knew I should have checked those posters before Robin and Nikki put them up, but I just didn't have time. The printer goofed!" She frowned. "Well, they'll just have to do it over. Let's hurry, Rick, I want to call them before classes start."

"I can't go any faster," Rick said. "For one thing, I'm behind a school bus, and I'm already going the speed limit."

Lacey groaned.

"Come on, relax," Rick said, reaching over to squeeze her hand. "We haven't been able to see each other much lately. Let's enjoy it while we have the chance, okay?"

Lacey smiled at him, but her mind was still on the posters. "Do you think the printer will do them over for free?" she asked anxiously. "I mean it really was his fault. And I don't know if I could talk Lenny into paying more money."

"I think—" Rick started to say.

"And then the new posters will have to go up," Lacey interrupted. She groaned. "How am I going to find time for all of this?"

Rick touched her hand again. "Do you think you could find some time for me?" he asked.

Lacey turned to him anxiously. "Oh, Rick, I'm sorry," she said. "I didn't mean to ignore you. I just have so much to do, and now this poster mix-up."

"I know," Rick said. "I don't mean to push you or anything. I miss you, though."

"And I miss you," Lacey told him.

They smiled at each other, and Lacey relaxed a bit. But by the time they arrived at school, her mind had started racing again. She leaned across the front seat and gave Rick a quick kiss. "Don't worry, it'll all be over soon, I promise."

Then Lacey jumped out of the car and ran toward the school so she could get to the telephone.

Rick sighed and shook his head as he opened the passenger door. He'd be glad when the Dead Beats finally came, but he'd be even gladder when they left.

Brittany had also seen one of the Dead Beats' posters on the way to school. Karen Jacobs was such a fool, she told herself. She'd said the group was coming to River Heights on Saturday. But there it was, in black and white: the Dead Beats would be in Platters on the seventeenth. That was Friday.

So. Karen had gotten it wrong. Good. She'd probably get plenty of other things wrong, too, and then DeeDee would be totally disgusted with her.

Brittany swept into school with a huge smile on her face.

Ten minutes later the smile had faded.

The first thing to change her mood was seeing Ben Newhouse, president of the junior class. He was walking slowly down the hall, arm-in-arm with his gorgeous girlfriend, Emily Van Patten. The two of them looked completely absorbed in each other.

Tall and good-looking, Ben was always after people to be on one committee or another. Since Brittany had met Jack, she hadn't been as involved as usual, but now she was ready to get started again.

She didn't really want to be on another committee, but it was important. Brittany's plan to combat Kim and Jeremy was to make herself even more visible than ever.

"Ben!" she called cheerfully.

"Uh, hi, Brittany." Ben stopped and waited for her to catch up to them. Emily looked impatient.

"I know Winter Carnival is ages away," Brittany told him. "But I have some great ideas for it. Why don't we get a committee going on it?"

"Well, thanks." Ben looked embarrassed. "It's just that, uh, we've already got a committee working on it."

"What?" Brittany didn't bother to conceal her surprise. "Why didn't you ask me to head it?"

Ben blushed and looked at his shoes. "Well, you've been kind of busy lately," he said. "I haven't seen you around school much, so I—"

Brittany kept her temper. "Well, I'm here now," she said sweetly. "So I can take charge."

Ben's blush deepened. "Thanks, but I couldn't ask the chairman to drop everything now." He paused. "But listen, we can use you, anyway. There's a meeting later this week. I'll get back to you about the time, okay?"

They could *use* her? She *headed* committees. She didn't come in at the last minute and do the dirty work.

Emily looked up at Ben. "We're all going to be late for class," she said significantly.

Brittany had to control herself. "See you around," she said shortly.

So, she thought, striding away. Kim was right when she said I was getting out of touch with school stuff. Well, let the Winter Carnival committee do without Brittany Tate.

In the meantime, there was Nikki Masters. Might as well get it over with, Brittany thought grimly. She'd interview that girl if she had to sit on her to do it.

But the minute Brittany made eye contact with her farther down the hall, Nikki turned pale.

She was around the corner and out of sight before Brittany could take another step.

What could possibly be the matter with Nikki? Brittany wondered. Or was something the matter with *her?*

Still standing in the crowded hall, Brittany gave her outfit a surreptitious glance. Her burgundy corduroy jeans seemed all right. No spots that she could see on her silky ivory blouse. What was it? Dirt on her face? A poppyseed from her breakfast roll stuck in her teeth?

Brittany started for her locker. She still

had about two minutes left before the bell. That's when she saw Erik Nielson, the blond cocaptain of the cheerleading squad. He was standing with Kim Bishop.

Naturally, Kim spun around and walked away. So did Erik.

Brittany tried to convince herself that Erik hadn't really seen her. He couldn't have. She and Erik were friends, but Erik had dated Kim, and *they* were friends, too, she remembered.

Deep inside, Brittany felt the beginnings of fear. Was Kim or Jeremy — or both — really going to ruin her at River Heights High?

The printer couldn't redo the posters. He said he'd refund the money, but they were tied up with an enormous order and couldn't get to Lacey's posters until Thursday. Neither of the other two printers in town could do a rush job, either.

It had taken Lacey all day, making frantic phone calls between classes, to get all this information. Now, after school, she stood outside with Nikki and Robin and delivered the bad news.

"What did Lenny say?" Robin asked.

Lacey shrugged. " 'Gee, tough break, Lace.' "

"That's all?" Nikki was indignant. "Doesn't he care?"

"Oh, he cares," Lacey said. "But he keeps saying this autographing session is my baby. I think he's convinced it'll never happen. But it's going to happen, you can count on that," Lacey added quickly.

"Of course it is," Nikki agreed.

"So what are you going to do about the posters?" Robin asked.

Reaching into her knapsack, Lacey pulled out a felt-tip marker. "I'm going to change the dates on the posters, what else?"

"*All* of them? That's a huge job," Nikki said. "It'll take you forever. Besides, you don't know every place Robin and I put them. Listen, I don't have rehearsal tonight. I'll help you."

"Me, too," Robin offered. "It's not exactly my idea of a good time, but it beats studying."

Lacey laughed and reached into her bag again. This time she came up with a whole fistful of markers. "I was hoping you'd say that!"

The three of them set out right away in Nikki's car. At first the job was easy. The stores where Robin and Nikki had put the posters up earlier in the week were open, and the owners helped by taking them down so they could change the date.

After dinner—burgers to go—things got harder. Some of the stores had closed by then, and Lacey had to write the owners notes.

"Why do I feel like I'm breaking a law or something?" she asked as she slipped one of her notes beneath the door of a bakery.

"Maybe because there's a police car sitting right across the street," Robin said. "And the two officers in it are watching us very closely."

Later the job got even harder. Nikki and Robin hadn't kept a record of where they'd put every poster.

"That's okay," Nikki said. "I know how many we put up. Seventy-five. I've been keeping track of how many we've fixed so far."

"How many?" Lacey asked.

"Forty-seven." She frowned. "Only twenty-eight more to go."

"Onward," Robin said.

At eight o'clock they still had twelve posters to go. They were all getting tired, Lacey could tell. But she was determined to finish the job and get it right. It *was* her baby, and she wasn't going to let anything happen to it.

"How about Bay Street?" she asked.

Robin nodded. "I'm pretty sure we put some up on a few of the buildings there."

They found three posters on Bay Street. That left nine.

Lacey was starting to feel guilty. "Listen,

you guys should go home. Thanks for all your help, but I can do the rest myself.''

"Sure," Nikki said wryly. "I'll just drop you off here in the dark, and you can wander around town alone the rest of the night.''

Lacey laughed. "Okay. Drive on, Nikki.''

Robin remembered four more posters they'd put up in a small shopping center on the outskirts of town.

"Seventy down, five to go,'' Robin announced.

The last posters were the hardest to find. After another half hour, they'd only found three. Then Lacey spotted one on a construction fence and hopped quickly out of the car. But as she was changing the date on the poster, a deep-throated rumble started up on the other side of the fence.

Suddenly the rumble changed to a fierce, bloodthirsty bark. An unseen dog hurled itself against the fence, growling and barking viciously.

Lacey was back in the car in two seconds. "That dog was going for my throat!'' she gasped.

"Let's get out of here before it chews its way through the fence and demolishes the car,'' Robin said, laughing.

At nine-thirty they decided to call it quits. There was just one more poster to go.

"We'll see it some time during the week," Nikki said as she stopped the car in front of Lacey's house.

"I know," Lacey said. "But I hate the thought of that one lonely poster with the wrong date on it hanging somewhere out there in the middle of River Heights."

"Don't worry about the poster," Robin told her with a grin. "Worry about the poor person who sees it and turns up at Platters on the wrong day."

"That couldn't really happen, though," Nikki said quickly. "I mean, the radio station is doing promotional spots, and Lacey took out ads in the newspapers."

"You're right," Lacey agreed. "A person would have to be totally out of it to get the day wrong."

Brittany and her mother didn't get home from Blooms until almost ten that night. Seven was the usual closing time on Mondays, but it was Ruby's day off, and the two of them had stayed late to fill last-minute orders.

"You know what I'd like?" Mrs. Tate asked, kicking off her shoes and sinking into a wing chair. "A big dish of ice cream. I'm too tired to move, though."

"I'll get it," Brittany offered. She was tired

too, but her mother deserved being waited on. "I think I'll have some myself."

Ice cream was on Brittany's forbidden list, but that night she didn't care. It had been an absolutely rotten day, and it was only Monday. If the rest of the week was anything like it, she'd need a little boost to keep her going.

She kicked off her own shoes and padded barefoot into the kitchen. Maybe she'd even splurge and have a diet soda ice cream float.

She'd just scooped some ice cream into a bowl for her mother when the phone rang. She almost dropped it when a voice said, "Hi, Brittany. It's Jack."

# 10

Brittany's heart leapt, but she managed to sound calm instead of desperately relieved. She was also furious that he hadn't called in so long, but she hid that, too. "Jack," she said. "It's nice to hear from you." Nice, nothing. It was fantastic. Finally, finally, *finally!*

Jack cleared his throat. "Yes. Well, I've been kind of busy."

"So how are things going?" Brittany asked, still very casual.

"Not bad. Pretty good, in fact."

And they're going to get much better, Brittany added silently. "Well—"

"Listen, Brittany," Jack broke in. "I'd like to talk but not over the phone."

I'll bet, she thought, smiling to herself. After all this time, we'll definitely need some privacy. "What did you have in mind?" she asked.

"How about if I pick you up tomorrow, sometime after dinner?" he suggested. "We can get some coffee or something."

"That sounds great, Jack," Brittany said.

"Good. I'll be at your house around seven o'clock."

"I'll be waiting."

After Jack said goodbye, Brittany did a little barefoot dance on the cool tile floor. It had been horrible without him, but she'd stuck it out.

Already thinking about what she would wear, Brittany put the ice cream away. She didn't need it anymore. She had Jack again, and this time, she was going to keep him.

When Lacey walked into Platters on Tuesday after school, she stopped and took a good look around. They'd need more space. They could hardly ask the Dead Beats to squeeze themselves into a corner or between a row of record bins.

"Lenny, we've got to clear out the front of the store," she announced. "We're short-handed today, so would you help me carry these stands of blank cassettes to the back?"

Lenny grinned as they lifted one of the stands. "What's the matter, Lace? You look a little nervous. Is this big promotion starting to get to you?"

Lacey made a face at him, even though she knew he was only teasing. But she *was* starting to feel a bit jittery. This was the most important thing she'd ever handled by herself and she wanted everything to be perfect. Everything. Even that single stupid poster she still hadn't found.

"I just want things to go smoothly, that's all," Lacey said. Then she remembered something. "Where did you put all the albums?"

Lenny looked blank. "What albums?"

"The Dead Beats' albums," Lacey replied, trying not to sound annoyed. "They were supposed to come in today, remember?"

"Nothing came in today except bills," Lenny informed her.

Leaving Lenny alone with the cassette stand, Lacey sped back into the office. She'd made arrangements the week before for those albums to be delivered. The record supplier had assured her they'd be here by today.

She dialed the supplier's number. He seemed as surprised as she did.

"I sent them out. Let's see," he said. Lacey heard some papers being shuffled.

"Yep, here it is. They went out last week, just like I promised. Should have been there by now."

Lacey's hand tightened on the receiver. "They're not."

"Well, I'll try to trace them," he said cheerfully. "You sit tight, little lady, and I'll get back to you."

Lacey managed to ignore the "little lady" part, but she couldn't sit tight. The whole point was to have the Dead Beats and the albums there together. People would come to see the group and get their albums autographed—the albums they'd bought in Platters.

While Lacey waited, trying not to chew her fingernails, she remembered once again the lone poster. It was really bugging her, like the slow drip of a leaky faucet.

If the albums couldn't be traced, she'd have much more than a leak on her hands. She'd have a flood.

Tuesday evening at seven-thirty, Brittany slid gracefully into a booth in a coffee shop at the edge of the Westmoor campus. She'd been hoping Jack would take her to Leon's. Most of the kids from River Heights High hung out there, and she wanted to be seen with him.

But she could hardly complain. They were

together again, that was what counted. They both ordered coffee, and it arrived almost immediately.

"You're looking good, Jack," Brittany said in her throatiest voice as soon as the waitress had left. Was he ever! A brown sweater to match his eyes, his hair so thick and shiny she wanted to bury her fingers in it.

Later, Brittany told herself. She waited, expecting him to return the compliment. She'd worn a soft midnight blue sweater, and she knew she looked sensational.

All Jack did was stir his coffee. When he finally did look up, his eyes weren't sparkling as they usually did. And instead of complimenting her, he said abruptly, "Brittany, it's time we broke it off."

Dustin! Brittany thought. He's still mad that I flirted with Dustin that time.

Tossing her head so her dark hair swirled around her shoulders, she laughed lightly. "Jack, you haven't been angry all this time about that silly tennis game?" She leaned forward and smiled. "To tell you the truth, I don't play tennis at all. And I — well, I flirted with Dustin to cover up."

"I figured that out," Jack said. "I also know you've been seeing Dustin."

All right, Brittany thought. He's not jealous. He's furious.

"Well, Jack, you didn't call me for days," she said, pouting prettily. "If you had, I would have explained everything to you. Did you really expect me to sit home and wait around?"

Jack said nothing.

"Dustin doesn't mean anything to me, Jack," Brittany told him. "I only went out with him because you didn't call."

Jack looked away. "Why *did* you go out with me, Brittany?"

"Why?" Didn't he know? "Because I—"

"Don't say you love me," Jack interrupted, holding up a hand. "You might think you do, but you don't. You might like the way I look and the fact that I'm older and that I belong to the country club." He broke off and frowned. "Why didn't you just tell me you didn't belong? Why did you put on that big act?"

Brittany was suddenly furious. "Who told you?" she asked. If it was Jeremy Pratt, she'd break his elegant nose.

Jack shrugged. "Some people who work at the club," he said. "Not on purpose; they kind of let it slip. But the way you treated people there, I wouldn't have blamed them if they'd snitched on you."

The way she *treated* people? Was he implying that she was a snob?

"You love money and looks and expensive things like the club," Jack went on. "It doesn't really make any difference who gives them to you. I couldn't believe it when you tried to keep me from knowing that your mother owns a flower store. What's the matter with that?" Sadly he shook his head. "You're not the girl I thought you were when we first met, Brittany."

"But I am!" she insisted. "I haven't changed a bit."

Jack shook his head. "Well, then, you're not the girl I want."

It was time to pull out all the stops. Leaning across the table, Brittany took one of his hands. "Have you forgotten how it was, Jack?" she asked softly. "All those times when we were so—close?"

"I haven't forgotten anything, Brittany." Slowly, Jack pulled his hand away and met her eye. "It's over between us, Brittany. I'm seeing another girl."

It wasn't time to panic yet, Lacey told herself the next day. It was only Wednesday, and she had until Saturday. She was going to stay calm.

When the record supplier in Chicago had called her back the past night, he still hadn't discovered what had happened to the Dead

Beats shipment. But he was hopeful that he could. In the meantime he repeated to Lacey that she was to sit tight.

She didn't have much choice, she thought glumly. There she was, stuck in social studies. At least they weren't having a pop quiz.

The minute the class was over, Lacey dashed from the room and over to the main entrance, where there were two pay telephones. Feeding in some change, she dialed the record store.

"Platters," Lenny answered after five rings.

"It's me," Lacey said quickly. "Any word?"

"Nope," Lenny said, raising his voice over the music in the background. "I'm starting to think this whole promotion thing is jinxed."

"Why are you always so pessimistic?" Lacey asked, annoyed.

"Look, I've got a customer," Lenny said. "I'll see you later, okay?"

Sighing, Lacey said goodbye and hung up. Whirling around, she almost crashed into Rick.

"Hey, what's wrong, Lace?" he asked, seeing the look on her face.

Lacey groaned. "What isn't?" She quickly told him the story. "Unbelievable, huh?" she said when she finished.

Rick put an arm around Lacey's shoulder. "Come on," he said. "Worrying's not going to help. I'll tell you what, let's go to Leon's after school. Then we can talk about it over pizza. Together."

"That'd be great," Lacey said. "But I can't today, Rick. There's a student council meeting after school and I've got to be there."

Rick shook his head. "Look, Lacey, I know you've got a busy schedule and all, but I thought I was part of your life, too."

Lacey looked at him in surprise. "You are, Rick," she told him. "You know you are. And as soon as this whole Dead Beats thing is over, everything will be back to normal. *I'll* be back to normal." Laughing, she took his hand and squeezed it. "Just wait, Rick Stratton. In a few days, you won't be able to get rid of me."

Rick laughed and shook his head. Lacey had already taken off down the hall again.

When things had gone wrong in the past, Brittany had always been confident that she could make them work out. But when she went to school on Wednesday, still reeling from Jack's news, she wasn't so sure she could.

The things he'd said! He'd all but called her a social climber! Maybe she *did* like the finer things in life, but that didn't mean she wasn't crazy about Jack. If she'd only been interested in what a guy could give her, she would have gone after somebody like Jeremy Pratt.

Brittany thought she'd reached the low point of her life the night before, when Jack had told her they were through. But by noon the next day she realized the low point wasn't even in sight. By then, the news was all over school: Brittany Tate and Jack Reilly had split up.

Brittany had hoped to keep the breakup a secret until she could come up with a good story about why it happened. No such luck, though. Jeremy Pratt stopped her as she was heading toward the cafeteria.

"What do you want now, Jeremy?" Brittany snapped. "I thought you wouldn't even risk being seen with me."

"True," he said, sneering. "But I wanted you to know that I ran into Jack Reilly at the club last night. He was having a late dinner with a very pretty girl, and they seemed to be having a great time."

Brittany was speechless. Jack had actually gone to the club with that other girl — whoever she was — after he'd tossed Brittany away like an old shoe!

"Jack didn't tell me what happened between you two, naturally," Jeremy went on.

"But I thought the least I could do was offer you my condolences."

Brittany finally found her voice. "Get a life, Jeremy."

So Jeremy was the one who had spread the news. It was bad enough that Jack had broken up with her, Brittany fumed. But knowing that everyone was talking about it made things even worse. The only bright spot was that no one knew the details.

"Tell me everything," Samantha gushed later in the day. Her voice was sympathetic, but her eyes were filled with curiosity.

Brittany had managed to avoid Samantha until then, but her friend had finally cornered her in one of the bathrooms.

Leaning toward the mirror, Brittany slicked on a fresh coat of lipstick. "There's not much to tell, really," she lied. "We just decided that it was time for both of us to move on."

"Oh?" Samantha's eyes narrowed. "I seem to remember you telling me just the other day that Jack was busy with some history project."

History. Brittany almost gagged. The only thing Jack had told her about his new girl-friend was that they'd gotten to know each other working on the history project. He hadn't said any more, and that was fine with

Brittany. At the moment she didn't want to hear about the other girl; it was bad enough that she even existed.

"Yes, that *is* what I told you," she admitted to Samantha. "That's what Jack and I decided to say."

Samantha didn't look convinced. "Why?" she asked bluntly.

Brittany smoothed her eyeshadow with a fingertip. "Because we didn't want people to think we'd had a big fight or anything. We didn't. We just kind of—drifted apart." She smiled ruefully into the mirror. "You know how it is."

"Mmm." Samantha looked thoughtful. "Are you sure this new ladylove of his didn't make Jack drift?"

The new ladylove could drown, for all Brittany cared. "Of course I'm sure," Brittany said.

Samantha frowned. "You don't seem too broken up about any of this."

"Broken up? Well, I'm not thrilled, of course. It's always a bit sad when a relationship ends." Brittany stood back from the mirror and examined her eyes. She was surprised they weren't still puffy from crying the night before. The ice packs must have done the trick.

Brittany looked Samantha straight in the eye. "How can I pretend to be brokenhearted?" she asked with a sly smile. "I've got Dustin Tucker waiting in the wings, remember?"

Samantha laughed, shaking her head in admiration, and Brittany knew she'd bought the story. It was one of the hardest acting jobs Brittany had ever done, but she'd managed to pull it off.

And she *did* have Dustin, she reminded herself. He was good-looking and fun, and he definitely liked her. Life was pretty bad at the moment, but it wasn't totally bleak.

# 11 ~

"Just think," Nikki said eagerly. "In two more days the Dead Beats will be right here in River Heights! Live!"

Tim laughed as they walked down the hall together on Thursday morning. "You're really excited about them, aren't you?" He grinned. "So which one's your favorite?"

"Jake Blackstone," Nikki answered immediately. "He's fabulous."

"You mean he's a fabulous drummer or he's fabulous looking?"

"Both." Nikki laughed. She took Tim's hand and squeezed it. "His eyes are brown, though," she said with a smile. "I only fall in love with guys who have gray eyes."

Tim laughed. "That's nice to know. Uh-oh," he said suddenly. "I see a stormy-eyed redhead coming our way."

"Oh, no," Nikki said. Lacey was hurrying down the hall toward them. "I have a feeling she's not bringing good news."

Lacey's light blue eyes *were* stormy, and her hair was loose, flowing around her shoulders in a mass of curls that bounced with every furious step she took.

Nikki was right. The news was not good.

"You won't believe this!" Lacey announced. "The records are lost!"

"Lost?" Nikki cried. "How could that happen?"

"Nobody knows," Lacey replied. "And nobody knows where they are now. They'll probably wind up in Timbuktu."

"Can't you order more?" Tim asked.

"Not from the same guy," Lacey moaned. "He doesn't have any more in stock. Even if he did, they wouldn't get here in time." She slumped against a bank of lockers, looking gloomy for a moment. Then she straightened up and started pacing. "If only there was something I could do! It's so frustrating when things go wrong and there's nothing you can do about it!"

"I think I might be able to help," Tim added thoughtfully.

Lacey and Nikki turned to him. "How?" they both asked.

"Remember my friend in Chicago, Carl Schmidt?" Tim said. "His dad's a record distributor. Why don't I give him a call? Maybe they've got the albums in stock."

Lacey's eyes lit up. "Would you? Oh, Tim, that'd be great!" She fished in her purse and brought out a handful of coins. "Here. Go call him now, okay? Please? I don't know how to thank you."

Tim chuckled. "Just keep Nikki away from Jake Blackstone, that's all I ask." He gave Nikki a quick kiss and went off to make the call.

By noon Tim had an answer: Carl's father did indeed have the albums in stock in his Chicago warehouse.

Tim reported the good news to Lacey, Nikki, and Robin in the cafeteria. "Now all we have to do is get them here," he said.

"Can't they send them by overnight mail?" Robin asked.

"It would cost a fortune," Lacey told her, twirling the straw in her milk. "That many records weigh a ton." She took a sip of milk, thinking hard. "If I only had that car already, I'd drive to Chicago and get them myself! I probably wouldn't be able to bring them all, I guess, but I could get enough here for the signing. Carl's father would send the rest."

"Hey, why not?" Tim said, slapping his hand on the table. "Let's do that!"

The others stared at him.

"It'll work," he said. "Chicago's only—what? A three-hour drive from here?"

"Sure, but a three-hour drive in *what?*" Robin asked.

"How about my car?" Nikki suggested quickly. "We can get a lot of records in the trunk. My father has a luggage rack we could put on top, so we could get even more boxes up there. Tim and I can switch off driving." She gave him a light punch in the arm. "You'll come in handy for lifting the records, too."

"Lacey and I can navigate," Robin said, catching the spirit. "You're right, Tim. It'll work. We can leave tomorrow right after school, zip up to Chicago, get the records, and zip right back."

"Wait!" Lacey said, sounding very serious. "You guys forgot to ask *my* opinion about all this."

The others stopped talking and stared at her.

Lacey couldn't keep her solemn face on for long. Grinning from ear to ear, she said, "Chicago, here we come!"

"Brittany!" a voice called out in the hallway.

Brittany had to stop herself from visibly cringing. It was DeeDee Smith. She turned around slowly, trying to look pleasant. At least Karen "The Shadow" Jacobs wasn't around this time.

"What have you been doing these days, anyway?" DeeDee asked. "Hiding out?"

That would be nice, Brittany thought. "Of course not, DeeDee," she said smoothly. "If I haven't been to the *Record* office much lately, it's because I'm extremely busy. But as long as I get my column in, does it matter?"

"I guess not," DeeDee replied. "Not if your column is good," she added significantly.

Brittany's dark eyes widened. "What do you mean? What was the matter with it?"

"Come on, Brittany." DeeDee shook her head. "The column you turned in Tuesday was about *shoes.*"

"That's hardly the way I'd describe it," Brittany replied coolly. "I made comparisons between popular styles of shoes and the personalities of people who wear them. I thought it was rather clever myself."

"I might have, too," DeeDee told her. "Except you did the same thing with T-shirts about a month ago." She tilted her head and looked at Brittany carefully. "What's the matter, Brittany? Are you having trouble coming up with ideas? Why don't you talk to Karen? She usually has some good ones."

Brittany had to control herself. "Really, DeeDee, that won't be necessary," she said, forcing a light laugh. "I've got plenty of ideas."

She *was* having some trouble thinking up things to write about, but that wasn't the point. She'd do a column on meatloaf recipes before she went to Karen Jacobs for ideas.

"Besides," she went on, "the T-shirt column was a big hit, and the one on shoes will be, too. I——"

"Don't get in a snit, Brittany," DeeDee interrupted. "That's not what I needed to talk about anyway. I wanted to ask how the piece on the *Our Town* leads was coming."

"Oh, fine," Brittany lied. She still hadn't gotten to Nikki, but she'd decided to interview Tim first, anyway. Then she could ask him to light a fire under Nikki. "I'm really in a hurry, DeeDee. Anything else?"

"Just the interview with the Dead Beats," DeeDee said as Brittany turned to go. "You might not be able to get near them, but I want you to try. You know when they're coming, right? You won't forget?"

"The date's engraved on my brain," Brittany called over her shoulder. But before she had a chance to start fuming about DeeDee and her insults, she turned a corner and collided—hard—with Kim Bishop.

Both of them stepped back immediately.

"You should watch where you're going, Brittany." Kim's voice was icy.

"My eyes were wide open," Brittany replied.

"Well, I hope they stay that way," Kim told her as the two of them bent down to gather the books and papers they'd dropped. "Because pretty soon, you're not going to have any friends left here at school. So watch carefully."

Brittany laughed softly. "You don't have that much influence, Kim."

"Not alone," Kim agreed. "But Jeremy Pratt's not exactly on your side, either. I think the two of us can take care of you without much trouble. As a matter of fact, we've already started. Haven't you noticed?"

Brittany was trying to come up with a zinging reply when she suddenly realized that it was absolutely silent in the hallway. School had been over for five minutes. Why wasn't everyone stampeding for the door?

Still on her knees, Brittany glanced around. A group—no, a crowd—of kids had gathered. And every pair of eyes was riveted on the exciting little scene she and Kim had created.

Erik Neilson, Ben Newhouse, Emily Van Patten, Ellen Ming, the junior class treasurer, and lots of other people she knew. In the back was a smiling Jeremy Pratt. Was it her imagination? Or was everyone avoiding her eyes? Everybody seemed to be watching Kim as if they had to take their cues from her.

Slowly Kim stood up, chin high. Then she stepped neatly around Brittany as if Brittany were a bug she didn't want to squash with her expensive leather shoe. She walked off toward the main entrance.

Then everyone else began to move. To Brittany, it seemed as if they couldn't get away from her fast enough.

Cheeks flaming, Brittany got to her feet and headed toward the front doors. Voices buzzed around her, and she was positive that they were all talking about her.

Jeremy and Kim really *were* out to ruin her. Jeremy had said so, of course, but she hadn't taken him seriously. Kim was right —together, she and Jeremy might not be able to ruin her, but they could do plenty of damage.

What else could fate possibly have in store for her? How about a lightning bolt, just to finish things off?

Dustin didn't seem to notice that everything was wrong. Normally, Brittany expected any boy she was dating to pay strict attention to her every mood. But this time, she didn't care. In fact, she was grateful. The last thing she wanted to do was describe the humiliating details of her life.

He'd been waiting for her after school. Fortunately, the girls gathered outside on the steps were so impressed by Dustin's good looks that they didn't seem to care about his car. By then Brittany didn't care, either. She was just glad to escape, in anything.

Now they were at a busy hamburger place —not a River Heights High hangout fortunately. Nobody there knew her, so nobody could snub her. Dustin had been doing most of the talking, and Brittany was glad to let him. In fact, her mind was still so jangled she'd hardly heard two words he'd said. Brittany tried hard to tune back in.

Dustin was looking out the window and shaking his head. "Too soon for snow, but the fall can't last forever."

"No," Brittany agreed. "Pretty soon we'll be able to go skiing." She skied about as well as she played tennis, but she looked great in the outfits. She knew Dustin would, too. "You probably can't wait to get on the slopes."

"No way." He laughed. "I like to stay warm."

A cozy picture popped into Brittany's

mind—a rustic ski lodge, a roaring fire, snow swirling outside, and she and Dustin inside, keeping each other warm.

"So do I," she told him softly.

"Yeah," he said, smiling at her. "Too bad you're still in school. Otherwise I'd be tempted to take you with me."

"We can always ski on the weekends," Brittany purred.

Dustin's brown eyes looked confused. "What do you mean, ski?"

"Isn't that what we've been talking about?" Brittany asked, feeling a bit confused herself.

"I don't ski. I told you, I hate the cold."

Brittany frowned. "Then what were you talking about when you said you'd like to take me with you?"

"Haven't you been listening to anything I was saying?" Dustin asked, obviously annoyed.

All right, so she hadn't. "Never mind," Brittany said. "Tell me again."

"I was talking about the Caribbean. Island-hopping. You know, the resorts."

"What resorts?"

"The ones I'm going to," Dustin said, exasperated.

Brittany sat very still. "When?" she asked.

"I told you that, too," he said.

"Tell me again."

"Day after tomorrow—Saturday." Dustin leaned back in the booth and gazed out the window again. "Yeah, it's time to move on. The country club is getting boring. If I'm lucky, I'll get a couple of jobs teaching tennis down in the islands. If I don't . . ." He shrugged and grinned.

Brittany stood up, her eyes blazing.

"What's the matter?" Dustin asked.

"So you're going to follow the sun," Brittany said in a cold, furious whisper. "Well, at least you won't have to worry about losing your tan."

She gave him a scathing look and picked up her purse and books.

"Where are you going?" Dustin asked. "Hey, Brittany, wait!"

Brittany turned on him. "I'm going home and I'll walk."

"It's at least five miles!" Dustin protested.

"Better five miles on foot than another inch in that tin can you call a car," she told him. "And I hope the Caribbean gets hit by a blizzard this winter!"

Dustin Tucker, Brittany thought furiously as she flounced out of the restaurant, was nothing but a tennis bum. She should have known. That lightning bolt had struck, after all.

## 12

On Friday morning before school "Team Chicago" had a quick meeting on the quad. They'd all told their parents about the drive. Robin's parents in particular weren't too happy, but they'd finally agreed to let her go.

It was too bad Rick couldn't come, Lacey thought. But he had wrestling practice, and besides, there wasn't room in the car. He'd been disappointed, too, she knew. When this whole thing was over, she told herself, she and Rick were going to spend a *lot* of time together.

"Okay," Lacey said, "let's take inventory. Maps?"

"Two," Robin said, holding them up.

"Gas?"

Nikki nodded. "I filled the car up just before I got to school."

"Directions to the warehouse?"

"Got 'em." Tim waved a piece of paper. "I brought some coffee, too," he added, holding up a thermos and a stack of paper cups.

"Good," Lacey said crisply. "We don't want to have to stop on the way."

Robin laughed. "Lacey, you're acting like a drill sergeant," she said. "Relax. This is going to be fun."

As soon as her third-period class was over, Brittany hurried out of the school building and caught a bus to the mall. She'd have to miss lunch, but she wasn't hungry anyway. She wasn't sure she'd ever eat again.

She couldn't think about that now. First, she had to try to interview the Dead Beats. Then she'd decide what to do about the rest of her miserable situation.

Brittany was at the mall by twenty minutes to twelve. The autographing started at noon. The store would probably be packed already. Maybe she should have cut that last class.

Inside the main door of the mall, she stopped, whipped a small mirror out of her purse, and checked her makeup. After all, she'd be talking to the newest, hottest rock stars in the country. And they were all gorgeous males.

Satisfied that she looked perfect—which was quite an achievement, since her life was in shreds—Brittany headed toward Platters.

Except for a few shoppers meandering along, the hall outside the store was empty. Where were the lines? Where were the photographers? Now that she thought of it, the bus should have been crowded with kids skipping lunch to get there. Why wasn't the entire hall packed solid with people waiting to get in?

Amazed that she could even get near the store, Brittany pushed open the door.

Except for a dark-haired man behind the counter, who was reading a magazine and loudly cracking his gum, the place was empty.

"Excuse me," Brittany said.

The man looked up. "Sure," he said. "What can I help you find?"

"The Dead Beats."

"Don't have the albums yet," he told her.

"Not the albums," Brittany said. "The actual, live Dead Beats."

He grinned. "Sorry. I've had plenty of kids calling to ask if they could camp outside the store tonight, but the answer's no. You'll just have to come back tomorrow and take your chances with everybody else."

"Tomorrow?" Brittany whispered. She couldn't believe it.

"That's right," the man said. "Tomorrow at noon. Check the poster on the front window there."

In a daze, Brittany walked outside and looked. She was back in ten seconds.

"The poster says the seventeenth," she informed him. "That's today. Friday, the seventeenth."

Suddenly the man burst out laughing. "Well, what do you know? Lacey said there was one poster she didn't make the change on. It turned out to be the one in my window!" He chuckled some more, shaking his head. "That's some joke, isn't it?"

Brittany managed a weak smile. "Yes," she agreed. "It's a real killer."

Fifteen minutes after the final bell, Tim turned the Camaro onto the freeway heading out of River Heights.

"Chicago, here we come!" Robin shouted.

Nikki turned around in the front seat and grinned. "Just think, Lacey. In a few more hours we'll have the records, and in one more day you'll have your raise."

"Did Lenny say how much he'd give you?" Robin asked.

Lacey shook her head. "We didn't get to that yet," she said.

"Don't settle for anything puny," Robin advised. "After all, you're bringing the Dead Beats to River Heights. That ought to be worth a lot."

"I'd give a lot just to get around this truck," Tim muttered.

"Why can't you?" Lacey asked.

"None of the lanes are moving," he said. "Must be an accident or something."

Traffic wasn't slowing down for an accident, fortunately, but it was definitely slowing down. In ten minutes, it had come to a dead standstill.

"I don't get it," Tim said.

"I do. Look." Robin pointed to a sign that read, "Your Tax Dollars At Work. Highway Construction. Detour Ahead."

Tim muttered some more, but Nikki laughed. "Don't worry. It can't take forever."

The detour took an extra forty-five minutes, but finally they were free.

Not for long.

"More construction?" Lacey moaned as they slowed down again.

"'Right Lane Closed, 200 Feet,'" Robin read.

"It's a good thing the Dead Beats are flying to River Heights tomorrow." Lacey sighed. "If they tried to drive, they'd never make it."

"Don't worry, Lacey," Tim told her. "The

warehouse doesn't close until late tonight. It's not even four yet. We've got plenty of time."

"You're right," Lacey agreed. "I didn't mean to complain. That's the last you'll hear out of me. From now on, I'm just going to sit back and enjoy the scenery."

But as she looked out the window, Lacey couldn't help noticing that the scenery was beginning to get wet. It was starting to rain.

It was raining in River Heights, too, but Brittany couldn't have cared less. She was in her room, lying on her four-poster bed. If she had a choice, she would have stayed there for the rest of her life.

The mistake about the Dead Beats was the last straw. That gum-chewing guy in the record store had told her that every other poster around town had been changed days ago. But she'd never looked at any of them.

And why should she have? She already had enough on her mind. How was she supposed to know about a stupid printer's error?

Turning onto her back, Brittany stared at the canopy over her bed. Two weeks earlier, she'd had practically everything. Now Jack was gone, Dustin—the creep—was going, DeeDee was breathing down her neck, and Kim and Jeremy had turned against her.

Did she have anything left?

Brittany closed her eyes. Then she sat up quickly. There *was* something left. She didn't know how she'd get it, but she knew she had to try.

The rain was coming down in buckets. Tim had the windshield wipers on high speed, but it was like trying to see through a waterfall. He had to slow down.

"Don't even try to hurry," Lacey told him. "Nothing's worth getting into an accident for, not even the Dead Beats."

"I don't really have a choice, anyway," Tim said. "It looks like the highway's flooded up ahead."

"Another detour?" Robin asked.

"If we're lucky," Tim replied grimly.

But there was no detour set up, and they had to crawl along with the rest of the cars, hoping the brakes would work when they finally got out of the flooded area.

Lacey told herself firmly not to worry. The worst that could happen was that they'd get back to River Heights later than they planned.

At last they were through the flooded part of the highway. It was still raining, but Tim was able to drive faster. Finally, at nine o'clock, they saw the skyline of Chicago.

Lacey breathed a sigh of relief. "We made it!" she cried.

She and Robin unfolded the city map and started giving directions to the warehouse. But the map was hard to read, and they made several wrong turns. It took Tim almost an hour of tense driving before they finally reached their destination.

The warehouse was a big, one-story building with a huge parking lot on one side. The lot was completely empty.

As soon as Tim stopped the car, all four of them jumped out into the rain and ran to the warehouse. They tried the main door, the loading doors, and even checked around back, just to make sure. But it was obvious the minute they drove up: the warehouse was locked and closed for the night. It was now ten o'clock.

"Hang on," Tim said. "There's a phone booth at the end of the street. I'll go call Mr. Schmidt and see if he can send somebody down here."

Pulling the hood of his windbreaker over his head, he dashed down the street.

The girls pulled their hoods up, too, and stood huddled together in the rain. After driving for so long, nobody wanted to get back in the car. No one said a word.

In a few minutes Tim came trotting back.

"Nobody home at the Schmidts'," he reported.

"You can try again in a little while," Nikki said.

Tim shook his head. "I just remembered something while the phone was ringing." He looked at Lacey. "Mr. Schmidt told me they'd be out of town for the weekend. They probably left today."

For a moment Lacey felt like crying, but she stopped herself quickly. She'd worked too hard to let a locked-up warehouse stop her now.

"Okay," she said crisply. "I've got a plan. The first thing we do is call our parents."

"What do we tell them?" Robin asked.

"That we're all safe and sound. And"— she paused—"that we won't be back in River Heights until tomorrow."

Nikki raised her eyebrows. "We won't?"

"No," Lacey told her.

"My parents will *kill* me," Robin groaned.

Lacey looked at her friend sympathetically. "I'm really sorry, Robin. But maybe they'll understand. I mean, we don't have enough money for a motel, but we don't have to tell them that. We can stay in the car tonight so we'll be here the second this place opens in the morning. It's only a few hours. Then we'll head back—with the records."

Lacey glanced around at the others. "So are you guys with me or not?"

Nikki, Tim, and Robin exchanged glances. "Of course we are," Nikki said. "You don't even have to ask."

Lacey gave them all a hug. "I couldn't have done this without such great friends," she told them. "Thanks for sticking by me."

"No problem," Robin said breezily. Then she grinned. "Besides, you're stuck with *us,* remember? All night. In a Camaro."

**13**

"Robin?" Lacey whispered. "What time is it?"

Robin squinted at her watch. "One-thirty."

"Oh. Do you think you could move your legs?"

"Only if I stick them out the window," Robin whispered back.

"You don't have to be so quiet," Tim said from the front seat. "Nikki and I are wide-awake."

"That's not why I was whispering." Lacey giggled. "I didn't want to interrupt any romantic moments up there."

"What romantic moments?" Nikki said dryly. "This stupid gearshift is poking me in

the side and Tim won't move over any farther.''

"I *can't* move over any farther," he protested. "If I did, I'd be out of the car."

"I know, let's all get out and stretch,"
Robin suggested. "Then we can switch seats
when we get back in."

It was raining harder than ever, but after
almost four hours in the car, nobody cared
about getting wet. Like characters in a
speeded-up movie, the four of them
jumped out, ran around the car a few
times, and jumped back in. They were totally
drenched, and now the inside of the car
was, too.

"We shouldn't have done that," Lacey
said. "We've gotten the seats all wet."

"Too late now," Tim said. "How much
time did we kill?"

Robin wiped off her watch. "A minute and
a half," she said. "Time flies when you're
having fun."

"Tim?"

"What?"

"There's a light over there," Robin said.

Tim turned his head; his neck was stiff.
"Patrol car, probably," he said groggily.
Then he snapped awake. "Uh-oh. We'd better
drive around the block a few times. There's

no way anybody would believe what we're doing here, and the Schmidts aren't home to vouch for us.''

As quickly as possible, Robin scrambled over the front seat. Nikki was still sound asleep. Tim slid up from the back, his knee colliding with Lacey's head.

"Sorry about that," he said.

Tim drove around several blocks until they were sure the patrol car was out of the neighborhood. Then he pulled back into the parking lot.

"That was kind of exciting," Robin said, checking her watch. "But it's only three-thirty. Let's do it again at four."

"We can't," Tim told her. "We don't have much gas left. We'll have to fill up the tank in the morning, so we'd better save what we've got for the trip to the gas station.''

Lacey cracked the windows for a little air, and the four of them settled down again.

"Is anybody asleep?" Nikki asked later.

"No," the other three mumbled grumpily.

"Has anybody slept at all?"

"No. Just you," Robin replied.

Nikki sat up, stretching as best she could. It was only five o'clock. "Let's take a walk," she suggested. "Just to the end of the block and back.''

"We did that already, when the rain let up," Robin reminded her. "Now it's pouring again. Besides, this neighborhood gives me the creeps."

"Is there any coffee left?" Lacey asked. "It's kind of cold in here."

"You've got to be kidding. The coffee was gone before we even reached Chicago," Tim said.

Everybody was quiet for a minute. Then Lacey said, "We could sing."

" 'Show me the way to go home,' " Robin sang in a dry, off-key voice.

They all laughed at that, and suddenly the car didn't seem so cold and cramped.

"I know," Tim said. "Let's play some car games. You know, the kind your parents made you play so you wouldn't keep asking if you were there yet."

"Good idea," Lacey said. "I'll start." She cleared her throat. "Okay, you have to guess who I am. Here's the first and only clue: I'm still living."

Robin grinned. "Are you sure about that?"

At seven-thirty, they were just starting in on Grandmother's Big Red Trunk when another car pulled into the parking lot.

"We did it!" Robin said. "We made it

through the night, and we're still friends!"

Groggy and stiff, the four of them tumbled out of the car and headed toward the man who had just arrived.

"Do you work here?" Tim asked.

"Sure do," the man replied. He looked them over curiously. "You wouldn't be the young people Mr. Schmidt told me about, would you? The ones wanting those rock records?"

"That's us," Robin said.

"You *do* have them, don't you?" Lacey asked anxiously. If he didn't, she'd sit right down on the asphalt and howl.

"Sure do," the man said again. "They're right inside. I was expecting you last night, actually. It kind of surprised me when you didn't show up."

"Not as much as it surprised us," Lacey said, laughing with relief.

After that, things went smoothly. The man helped them load the records into the trunk and onto the luggage rack. Then he directed them to the nearest gas station. It was Saturday, so they didn't have to worry about rush-hour traffic, and they were on the freeway by eight-fifteen. Even the weather was on their side. As they started back toward River Heights, the clouds finally broke and the sun shone through.

"This calls for some tunes," Tim said, switching on the radio.

"Good morning, Chicago," the radio announcer blared. "Here's one to start your day — number six on the charts and climbing fast. It's the Dead Beats with 'Come and Get It!'"

Robin burst out laughing. "They should dedicate that song to us," she said.

Brittany arrived at the mall at nine-thirty. She'd definitely gotten the right day this time. The place was jammed.

Holding up a notebook and her school ID card, she nudged her way through the crowd. "Press!" she called. "Let me through, I'm with the newspaper!"

She didn't bother to say which newspaper, and nobody questioned her. Both River Heights papers had people there, and so did the local television station.

Besides, Brittany thought, in her red wool suit and cream satin blouse, she probably looked at least five years older. Her rich dark hair was pulled back in a stylish knot, and her makeup was perfect. No one would have guessed that her life was a total mess at the moment.

And if things went the way she wanted, they'd never need to know, she told herself. Her plan wasn't going to be easy to pull off, she knew. But she had to try. It was the only hope she had left.

Luck had stayed with "Team Chicago" on the drive back to River Heights. They hadn't hit a single roadblock, detour, or flood. A twenty minutes to twelve, Tim screeched to a halt outside the back entrance of Platters.

"'We'll have to get Lenny to help us bring in the albums," Lacey said as they all leaped from the car.

She banged on the back door, and Lenny opened it a few seconds later. "You did it?" he asked her.

"We did it!" Lacey cried, and the four of them practically fell through the door.

Inside, Lacey came to a sudden stop, with the others bumping up behind her.

There, gathered in Lenny's office, were the Dead Beats: Jake Blackstone, the drummer; Tyler Holt, lead guitar; Sam Mazelli, bass; and Billy Bozeman, keyboard. All four of them. Live.

Lacey looked down at herself. She was wearing still-damp jeans, a dark blue sweater, and a yellow windbreaker. The Dead Beats were all wearing jeans, T-shirts, and worn leather vests, but they were *supposed* to look that way. Lacey was filthy and rumpled, her hair was loose and tangled, and she could still feel creases in her face from the car's upholstery.

Pushing her hair out of her face she gave the Dead Beats a beautiful smile. "Welcome to River Heights," she said, holding out her hand. "I'm Lacey Dupree."

Outside the front of the store, kids were standing three deep, just as Lenny had hoped. The crowd had almost erupted into pandemonium a few times, but four additional security officers soon arrived. They managed to get everyone into a line that snaked down the hall and around the corner to the main doors of the mall.

Brittany had staked out a space for herself right at the front of the line, and nothing had budged her. Not even the twenty-five-dollar bribe from one of her sister's pimply friends.

Scanning the crowd, she finally spotted them: Samantha and Kim, then Jeremy, three people behind them. They were way down the line.

Perfect, Brittany thought, smiling to herself. She knew Kim and Jeremy were still mad at each other, and even more furious with her, but she was going after them, anyway. They were the only two people who could possibly sponsor her for membership in the River Heights Country Club. That membership was the only thing that mattered to her now. It would be the first step on her climb back to the top of the social ladder.

Raising her notebook above her head, Brittany called into the crowd, "I'm with the press! I'd like to interview a few of you before the doors open — get your thoughts on meeting the Dead Beats live."

Hands shot up and voices called out. Brittany pretended to consider them all, but naturally, she pointed out Kim, Jeremy, and Samantha. Kim and Jeremy were both scowling at her, but that didn't matter.

"Make room for these people, please!" Brittany shouted. "We don't have much time. You three, come up here now!"

Grudgingly, the crowd made way for Samantha, Kim, and Jeremy. As soon as they reached her, Brittany whispered, "I really am going to interview you. And I'll make sure it takes a long time. That way, you guys will be right up front when the doors open."

"You sneaky thing!" Samantha whispered back, laughing. "I owe you one, Brittany. Thanks."

Brittany took a deep breath and looked at Kim and Jeremy. They were standing as far apart as possible, which was only about six inches. She saw them exchange a quick glance.

Neither of them thanked her, but Brittany

knew that neither of them was about to leave her side, either.

Inside the office, Lacey had introduced her friends to the Dead Beats and was just finishing up the saga of their race for the records.

"That's an incredible story," Jake Blackstone said, shaking his head. He was as good-looking as Nikki had expected—tall and lanky, with wavy brown hair and a gold stud earring. He didn't compare to Tim, though.

"I've got a question, Lacey." Tyler Holt, the lead guitarist, swung back his long blond hair and smiled at her. "Was it all worth it? Not that we're not glad to be here, I mean. It was a terrific idea you had, inviting us here. But you went through an awful lot to make this happen."

"You're telling me!" Lacey laughed. "Of course it was worth it. See, I made a deal with my boss." She looked at Lenny, who swallowed hard. "He said if I could get you into his record store, he'd give me a raise."

"She's saving for a car," Robin added.

Sam Mazelli grinned. "Well, Lenny? How about it? I'd say Lacey earned that raise, wouldn't you?"

Lenny nodded. "She's got it."

"Wheels, here I come!" Lacey cried.

"In fact, she's got a little extra, too,"

Lenny said. Reaching into his shirt pocket, he pulled out a white envelope and handed it to Lacey.

"What's this?" she asked.

"A cash bonus," he told her. "You'll have that car sooner than you think."

Everyone in the office started clapping, and Lacey threw her arms around her boss and gave him a hug. Lenny blushed and checked his watch.

"Okay, guys. One minute and counting," he announced. "Let's get this show on the road."

As soon as the crowd got a glimpse of the Dead Beats stepping from the office into the store, a huge roar went up. Then the manager pulled open the door, and three reporters dashed inside, one with a minicam. Flashes went off as they started firing questions.

When the front door had opened, Brittany was one of the first people through. Those outside were pushing forward, jockeying for position, but she made sure that Samantha, Kim, and Jeremy stayed with her.

"You three get ahead of me," she said quickly. "I can get this interview just by listening to the Dead Beats answer the other reporters. Go on!"

Flushed with excitement, Samantha stepped ahead of Brittany.

Jeremy came next. He didn't smile. But he touched two fingers to his forehead in a sort of salute. Brittany knew she couldn't expect any more. Not yet.

Kim came last. Brittany held her breath. Kim was looking stonily ahead, but as she passed, she gave Brittany a quick nod.

That was all. It wasn't much, Brittany knew. But it was a start, at least. With luck, she and Kim would be friends again soon. Then Jeremy would fall in line, and she'd have that club sponsorship in no time.

Things were beginning to look up. Finally.

Inside Platters, the chatter and shouts were almost deafening, and it had only been three minutes since Lenny opened the doors.

Lacey spotted Rick and Calvin and managed to hustle them inside. She was laughing and excited, until she saw Nikki's face.

A reporter had his camera up, ready to take a picture of the crowd, and Nikki threw her hand up to shield herself. The flash went off. With a small gasp, Nikki whirled around and started to edge toward the office door.

Lacey looked at Robin. They didn't have to say anything. Both of them knew that cameras and reporters still brought back painful memories for Nikki.

The day was ruined for Nikki, Lacey thought sadly. But the next wave of kids had pushed into the store, ready to buy albums and get the Dead Beats' autographs. Lacey had to help at the desk.

"You can talk to Nikki later," Robin said, practically shouting over the noise. "Go ahead. I'll find her. This is your day, Lacey!"

Giving herself a shake, Lacey headed uneasily back to work. Was she letting Nikki down after all Nikki had done for her? Or was she just imagining how upset Nikki had seemed? But she couldn't think about that now. She had a job to do.

------

**The school play is about to open, and Nikki's nerves are just about shot. But if she lets Tim down, will he fall for her understudy? Kim and Jeremy are determined to wreck Brittany socially. Can Brittany recharge their romance *and* persuade them to sponsor her for the country club? Find out in River Heights #5, *Between the Lines*.**